Suddenly, the Game Turned into a Duel.

Their eyes met, and an electric current shot through Jacquelyn. Scott's blue eyes searched her face, but their intensity penetrated deeper into her being. What was it Scott wanted to know? She wanted nothing more than to grant any request he would make of her. Her heart had stopped in her chest, and her blood had halted in her veins, because she felt sure Scott was going to kiss her. Her soul longed for his embrace. She was caught up in a magic spell of enchantment that she wanted to last forever.

PATTI BECKMAN's
interesting locales and spirited characters will thoroughly delight her reading audience. She lives with her husband Charles and their young daughter along the coast of Texas.

Dear Reader:

Silhouette has always tried to give you exactly what you want. When you asked for increased realism, deeper characterization and greater length, we brought you Silhouette Special Editions. When you asked for increased sensuality, we brought you Silhouette Desire. Now you ask for books with the length and depth of Special Editions, the sensuality of Desire, but with something else besides, something that no one else offers. Now we bring you SILHOUETTE INTIMATE MOMENTS, true romance novels, longer than the usual, with all the depth that length requires. More sensuous than the usual, with characters whose maturity matches that sensuality. Books with the ingredient no one else has tapped: excitement.

There is an electricity between two people in love that makes everything they do magic, larger than life—and this is what we bring you in SILHOUETTE INTIMATE MOMENTS. Look for them wherever you buy books.

These books are for the woman who wants more than she has ever had before. These books are for you. As always, we look forward to your comments and suggestions. You can write to me at the address below:

Karen Solem
Editor-in-Chief
Silhouette Books
P.O. Box 769
New York, N.Y. 10019

PATTI BECKMAN
Forbidden Affair

Silhouette *Romance*
Published by Silhouette Books New York
America's Publisher of Contemporary Romance

SILHOUETTE BOOKS, a Simon & Schuster Division of
GULF & WESTERN CORPORATION
1230 Avenue of the Americas, New York, N.Y. 10020

ISBN: 0-671-57227-X

First Silhouette Books printing June, 1983

10 9 8 7 6 5 4 3 2 1

Map by Ray Lundgren

America's Publisher of Contemporary Romance

Printed in the U.S.A.

Other Silhouette Books by Patti Beckman

Chapter One

The evening was muggy with a humidity peculiar to New Orleans early in summer, when gathering tropical storms in the Gulf of Mexico bring an ominous weight to the air. Rain began to fall at sundown, glistening on the broad leaves of banana trees in the ancient flagstoned courtyards of the Vieux Carre. It sizzled on shingled rooftops and brought steam swirling up from the narrow streets that were still hot from the day's sun.

The night life of the French Quarter was beginning as Jacquelyn La Salle walked from the broad, twentieth-century bustle of Canal Street into the historic setting of the Old World. Tables at Arnaud's and Galatorie's were becoming crowded. Neon illuminated dripping seventeenth-century balconies and iron grillwork where, in another century, gaslights had dispelled the darkness. The rain spattered on the cobblestones. A horse-drawn carriage clip-clopped by on the wet pavement. A few blocks over, on Bourbon Street, a jazz band was playing its first number of the evening.

As Jacquelyn stepped from the curb, her thoughts and attention drawn to the surrounding architecture, she heard the squeal of brakes. Smoking rubber clawed at the street wildly. From the corner of her eye she caught a flashing glimpse of a deadly mechanical monster bearing down on her.

Some primitive instinct, operating a split second before conscious thought, caused her to leap back, taking a glancing blow instead of the full, deadly impact of the black automobile that had threatened to snuff out her life instantaneously.

In the quiet hours close to dawn, Jacquelyn regained consciousness briefly in the room of a hospital. She heard a soft moan and then realized it was her own voice. The white cap of a nurse appeared. Her smile was comforting.

"You're all right—just fine. . . ." the voice said reassuringly.

The pain came in a rushing throb. "I don't feel just fine." Jacquelyn moaned louder this time. A needle stung her arm before soft euphoria and sleep overcame her once again.

The next time she awoke, the room was lighter. Jacquelyn saw others in the room beside the nurse. A man in a white medic jacket, a doctor type, stood over her. At the perimeter of her vision. Standing a respectful distance from her bed was another man, a police type, she guessed.

The doctor was smiling cheerfully. *Go ahead and smile,* Jacquelyn thought crossly; *you're not lying here hurting and all broken up.* He said, "Well, Miss La Salle, for a young lady who got run over last night, you're in remarkably good shape. You don't have any broken bones that we can find. There are countless bruises, of course, and a slight concussion. The car must have struck you a glancing blow. You'll have to stay in bed for several days and you're going to be sore as a boil for a week or two, but then you'll be fine as new."

Jacquelyn felt the soreness radiating throughout her entire body. She tried to shift her position in the bed, but the sharp stabs of pain halted her movements. *"Un naufroge,"* she mumbled.

"What?"

"My father was Acadian," she explained. "That's an old bayou Cajun saying. Means an auto or buggy wreck. I guess it popped into my mind because the car made a wreck out of me."

The policeman moved closer to the bed. "Do you feel like talking, Miss La Salle?" he asked.

Jacquelyn was immediately sorry that she had encouraged him by her feeble attempt at levity. "No," she said frankly.

"Well, I just wanted to ask you if you could give us any kind of description of the car that hit you."

A vague memory flashed in Jacquelyn's mind. She recalled stepping off the curb, but the vision of the car roaring down on her was a hazy blur of anxiety overshadowed by a blissful obscurity that had wiped from her mind any recall of the terrible incident.

She shook her head, and then groaned when even that slight movement sent pain racing through her body. "I take it you don't know who ran me down?" she said.

"Hit-and-run. I'm Lieutenant Davidson of the

traffic division. We don't have much to go on, I'm afraid, if you didn't see the car."

Jacquelyn struggled to pull herself from her lethargy. It made her mad that someone could assault her body and leave her lying along the street for dead and not even stop to render aid. What kind of person hit a pedestrian and then fled from the scene?

"No other witnesses?" Jacquelyn asked. "There were people behind me on the sidewalk. . . ."

"They were some distance back, looking in a window of an antique shop. By the time they realized what happened, the car was disappearing down the street. A heavy black sedan, they thought. That's about all we know."

A wave of bitter disappointment rushed over Jacquelyn. She closed her eyes. She really didn't feel like discussing it.

The policeman got the hint and went away.

Jacquelyn slept for a while. Then the nurse woke her for lunch, which consisted of a bland soft-boiled egg, toast and Jell-O. Although her appetite had deserted her, Jacqueline forced down a few bites under the watchful eye of the nurse.

When the tray had been moved away, the nurse cranked Jacquelyn's bed up higher and announced, "You have a visitor. Shall I let him come in now? The doctor says it will be all right if you promise to go back to sleep afterward."

"Yes," Jacquelyn said. She felt sure it would be Austin D'Raulde—dear, faithful Austin, friend since childhood, and in love with her nearly that long. She looked around her for a mirror, hoping to find out what she looked like before Austin saw her. Then she recalled that the top of the hospital table usually had a place for cosmetics and a movable mirror. She flipped back the lid and gasped when she saw the dark circles under her large blue eyes. She ran her hand over her long brown hair to smooth it out into its usual straight style, but a few strands refused to lay flat. Well, she thought, what did she expect? She didn't really look too bad, considering she had recently been struck down by a hit and run driver.

The nurse whipped out the door, and then Austin came in with a rush, his arms loaded with flowers. His handsome dark features were deeply lined. His eyes looked almost frantic with worry. He gave Jacquelyn a long, troubled look.

"Austin, for heaven's sake," Jacquelyn said, trying for his sake to sound more cheerful than she felt, "it's not that bad. The doctor said I'd live."

Austin set the flowers down and took Jacquelyn's hand in his. He gripped her knuckles tightly. For a second, he was almost too choked up to speak. Then he said, "They found your identification in your purse and notified your Uncle Luther, and, of course, he called me right away."

"And you rushed up from Cypress Halls," Jacquelyn said softly, feeling a sudden rush of warmth for Austin.

"Of course." He glanced around the room. "Is there anything you need, Jacquelyn? Anything I can do?"

Jacquelyn shook her head, unable to speak the words. She experienced a sudden pang of guilt. Austin had always been so faithful, so loyal. It was obvious he cared for her. Why couldn't she feel the same way about him?

There was an awkward silence. "Uncle Luther and Hattie send their love," Austin went on. "They're pretty upset, as you can imagine. I'll call them right away and let them know how you are."

"Thank you, Austin," Jacquelyn said gratefully. It wasn't until this moment that she had thought about how concerned Uncle Luther and Hattie must be for her. They had been at home, thinking she was going about her normal duties, when a sudden phone call announced she had been the victim of a hit-and-run accident. They could not really know her true condition. They must have been terribly worried. "Tell them I'm coming along just fine," she said.

"Yes, I'll reassure them," Austin said. But his dark eyes looked deeply worried as he gazed at her. Then he turned to leave. "I'll be right back," he said. "I'm going to phone them now."

"I'm not going anywhere," Jacquelyn reminded him.

Austin gave her one last look before the door closed behind him. Jacquelyn rested back against the pillows on her bed. This was the first time in a long while that she had had time just to lie and think. Her schedule had been quite busy of late. But almost being killed in an unexpected accident gave one a different perspective on life. It seemed like a perfect time to review what she was doing and where she was headed.

She thought back over her relationship with Austin. He was her age, twenty-four, slender, wiry, with the dark good looks of his Creole French ancestry. He had been taken care of by her Uncle Luther after his father died. He had been educated at Tulane, had spent time in the army and now worked for Uncle Luther as his business manager.

Austin was an integral part of Jacquelyn's life as surely as was the bayou country of southern Louisiana where she had been born and had spent her childhood. She recalled some of the Cajun sayings of her father; the spicy Creole cooking of Hattie, Uncle Luther's maid, who had helped raise her; the legends of the Old South aristocracy on her Uncle Luther's side of the family; the superstitions and folklore of the bayou people. The whole of her past swirled in her mind like a huge cloud. And then her heart suddenly stopped when a face flashed in her memory—unruly light brown hair, blue eyes set in strong features. It was the face of Scott McCrann.

The door opened, breaking into her reverie, and Austin reentered the room.

"I told him you were on the mend," Austin said, smiling for the first time. "He seemed greatly relieved. He wouldn't take the doctor's word for your condition. He wanted to hear from me how you really are."

"That's just like Uncle Luther," Jacquelyn commented, smiling.

Austin edged over to the bed. Gently, he placed his hand over Jacquelyn's. She looked down at her covered hand lying on the bed sheet. She wasn't sure how she felt about Austin touching her in this way.

"Why not let me take you back to Cypress Halls for a visit?" he said softly. There was a pause. Jacquelyn looked at him, trying to read the meaning behind his gaze. "Your Uncle Luther would be delighted," he added, as if sensing her reluctance to let Austin get too close to her emotionally. "He's beginning to show his age, Jacquelyn, and he misses you. You're all the family he has now."

"I—I'll have to think about it," Jacquelyn said with hesitation.

"Because of Scott?" Austin asked pointedly.

Jacquelyn didn't answer. The knot in her throat made a reply impossible.

"I can tell you're tired," Austin said finally. "I better leave so you can get some rest. Is it okay if I come back this afternoon?"

"Sure," Jacquelyn said. "And thanks. It was so good seeing you. And the flowers are lovely."

"My pleasure," Austin replied.

When he had gone, Jacquelyn settled back on her bed, dimly wondering why she could not find it in herself to be more intimate with Austin. Sleep soon overtook her.

As if by prearranged design to back up Austin's invitation, a letter came from Uncle Luther the very next day, containing something of a mystery, designed, Jacquelyn was sure, to whet her curiosity and send her scurrying to Uncle Luther's side. The letter said in part,

My dear niece, I am deeply concerned about you. When I was notified of your accident, I immediately telephoned your doctor and he has assured me that you are not seriously injured and will be able to leave the hospital within a week. For this, I give thanks. Now I wish to invite you—no, plead with you—to return to Cypress Halls for a visit, so you may recuperate where you will be properly cared for. Also, I would like for you, while here, to consider what could well be the most important commission of your career. . . .

When Austin arrived at the hospital that day, Jacquelyn showed him the letter. "What on earth does he mean by that statement?" she asked. Since graduating from college, Jacquelyn had held a position as an interior decorator.

Austin smiled down at her. "Your Uncle Luther is not one to give his secrets away. I think I may have an idea, but you'll have to wait. I won't spoil his little intrigue."

"Austin! You know what an overgrown curiosity bump I have. Please."

"Nope. Sorry."

He laughed as he ducked to avoid the hospital pillow she threw at him. She was instantly sorry for her action as a dozen sore muscles ached.

At the end of the week, Austin took Jacquelyn to her apartment to pack some bags and make arrangements for Napoleon, her cat. Yes, she'd decided to return with him to Cypress Halls, she thought to herself with a certain degree of apprehension. It had not been an easy decision for her, either. Returning to her former home meant the danger of a close proximity to Scott McCrann. Inevitably, some painful wounds would be reopened. But perhaps it would be for the best. Seeing him again, she might at last put to rest the old hurt. Then she could get on with her own life once again as a whole person.

On the way to the apartment, Austin insisted they stop at the police station. Now, in broad daylight, with the shock of the hit-and-run accident beginning to fade, Jacquelyn could face talking about the incident. She went through the motions of reporting the sketchy details she could remember to the polite and concerned officer she was referred to. He wrote down a lot of information and asked many questions. Jacquelyn finally left with his assurance that they would investigate. But with so few clues to go on, she really didn't see what they could hope to accomplish.

When Jacquelyn entered her apartment, a chill raced up her spine. It was almost as if she were intruding on the abode of a stranger snatched at the last minute from the jaws of death. But that feeling quickly passed, and Jacquelyn packed her bags with a sigh of relief that it was she, and not a mourning relative, who was scouring through her closet and drawers.

"There now," she said. "Everything is taken care of, I guess. I notified the phone company to temporarily disconnect my service. I've got a leave of absence from my boss—I took care of all of that while I was still in the hospital. So I guess all I need to do now is see that Napoleon will be well cared for in my absence."

"Where is he, by the way?" Austin asked.

"My neighbor across the hall, Claudette Wilson, has him," Jacquelyn explained. "I called her from the hospital and asked her to look after him for a few days. She adores that cat. She's kind of a lonely soul. Frankly, I think she would like it if she could adopt Napoleon on a permanent basis. She feeds him chopped liver every day, so I don't think he would object in the slightest. His loyalty has a way of following where his stomach leads." Jacquelyn chuckled.

Jacquelyn crossed the hall and tapped at Claudette's door. It opened a crack, still on the chain, and a girl's eye peered out at her. "Oh, Jacquelyn."

She quickly released the chain and opened the door. "I'm so glad you're all right."

"I appreciated the flowers and the get well card, Claudette," Jacquelyn said. "It was sweet of you."

"I'm sorry I couldn't afford a larger bouquet," she apologized shyly.

Jacquelyn felt a sudden need to reassure Claudette, whose poor self-image stuck out like a red banner. "It was certainly the prettiest arrangement I received," Jacquelyn said.

Claudette blinked her eyes in surprise, and a soft smile stole across her face. The girl had moved in across the hall a couple of months earlier. She was slender, extremely pretty in a dark, haunting way, but she was quite shy and withdrawn. She seemed to have no friends at all. She wore a wedding ring and had told Jacquelyn her husband was overseas. Jacquelyn had felt sorry for her and had gone out of her way to be friendly. A few times she had invited the girl to go out to dinner with her. They had poked around antique shops and looked at the paintings on the sidewalk displays around Jackson Square, but they'd never really become close.

Once, when they were examining a piece of furniture in an antique shop, Claudette had revealed impulsively that she was a firm believer in reincarnation. She said she could remember previous lives quite well and that she had lived an earlier lifetime in this city a hundred years before and "died" in a yellow fever epidemic. Frankly, Jacquelyn had decided Claudette was a bit on the peculiar side, though certainly one of the most beautiful girls she'd ever met.

As Jacquelyn entered the girl's apartment, Napoleon sprang down from a couch and gave her leg a perfunctory rub of greeting. He was part Siamese—

at least he had the standard Siamese markings and the blue eyes—and it was certain he wouldn't have qualified in any pedigreed cat show. He had a great, fine tomcat head which bore the scars of many back alley fights. Jacquelyn had found him months ago on the walk outside her apartment building, half dead from an untreated puncture wound infection. She'd spent some thirty dollars on antibiotic shots at the vet and had nursed him back to health. Then he'd become her house pet, which apparently suited him fine. It seemed he'd arrived at the age in his tomcat career when he was content to settle down to a regular routine of good meals and a warm spot to sleep at the foot of Jacquelyn's bed.

"Claudette, I'm going to be away visiting my uncle for the next week or two. Would you mind very much boarding Napoleon?" Jacquelyn knew in advance what the answer would be. She was glad to be able to ask Claudette, because she knew it would make the girl feel important and would give her an opportunity to care for Napoleon full time.

"Oh, I'd just love to," she said, quickly picking him up and hugging him and rubbing his head with her cheek. "He's such good company. And no trouble."

Jacquelyn sensed that she was, in effect, giving Napoleon to Claudette. When she returned, the bond between the two would be so strong, how could she have the heart to insist on getting the cat back? It was just as well, she thought. Claudette needed Napoleon.

"I want to pay you for his food, of course," Jacquelyn said, taking some bills from her purse.

"Oh, no. I wouldn't hear of it," Claudette protested, pushing her hand away. "I'm just happy you weren't seriously injured. I hope you enjoy your visit. I'll keep Napoleon as long as you wish. Don't worry about him."

Jacquelyn smiled knowingly to herself. So it was done. Without speaking the words, they both understood that the cat now belonged to Claudette. Jacquelyn told Napoleon good-bye, rubbed his large head with her hand, and admonished him to be good. Her leaving didn't appear to tear the cat up very much, she thought wryly.

That matter taken care of, Jacquelyn followed Austin down the stairway of the Vieux Carre apartment building, across a small courtyard, and out to the street where his car was parked. He put her suitcase in the trunk. Soon they had left the city behind as they crossed the Huey Long Bridge and were headed south on Highway 23.

The afternoon grew old and the warmth of the September sun died. Gray shadows of dusk began staining the silent depths of the swamps. Bone white, draped in cloaks of dripping Spanish moss, the bare arms of swamp cypress trees were raised in mute and endless supplication toward lead-colored skies. A wraithlike mist was rising above the dark waters.

Jacqueline sat silently in the car next to Austin, the sight a foreboding reflection of her inner emotions. It had been so very long since she had allowed herself to think of Scott McCrann. She had tried to bury her feelings for him under a bustle of constant activity, keeping her mind so busy she had no time or energy left over to brood over him. She had told herself she had buried forever any attachments to him. But speeding along the highway in a direction she knew would eventually bring her close to him, she had to admit she had lied to herself.

Following the convolutions of the winding bayou, the road brought Jacquelyn and Austin at last to the oak-fringed entrance of Cypress Halls' grounds. She gazed down that mile-long tunnel that led under an archway formed by hundred-year-old trees to the time-ruined mansion. Her childhood had been spent in the isolated world that existed beyond those tireless oak sentinels.

Again she thought about Scott McCrann, also a part of that isolated world. How she was going to cope with the emotionally charged situation of being so close to him again, she was not sure. Maybe it had been a mistake to agree to return here.

She drew a deep breath as the car proceeded down the ancient private roadway that had known the shuffle of chained slaves, the rumble of ox-drawn sugarcane wagons and the marching of Civil War troops. No matter how many times she had seen the neglected plantation house where Uncle Luther lived, she was never quite prepared for it. It almost had a personality of its own, an overpowering character that always made it difficult for her to leave once she had returned.

When Austin's car emerged from the oak-shadowed drive, there it stood, a mansion still recalling the days of its bygone splendor. Cypress Halls. In a dying burst of color, the final rays of the September sun tinged the columns, galleries and wings in a soft diffusion of rose tints. Great sweeping shadows stretched over the gardens behind the structure, while pockets of darkness multiplied in the recesses of the galleries, doorways and windows.

Without even realizing that she was once again coming under the spell of the house, Jacquelyn smiled and thought about this great old structure in bygone days. Here, many lives had been lived out, many love affairs consummated and broken, and many fortunes lost and made. She could easily have been convinced that right now, the shadowy forms of plantation belles in hooped skirts could be seen behind the paint-thin shutters. She imagined hearing faintly the music of the quadrille from the ballroom.

The architecture of Cypress Halls was the classic Louisiana Creole style, composed of Greek Revival and Georgian influences cast in the mold of its own time and location. The great Ionic columns, like the last desolate outposts of an army long since gone, stood in solemn dignity against the ravages of time and weather. But chipping masonry, a broken window here and there and a garden spotted with weeds admitted to a recent era of neglect, forced on the owner, Uncle Luther, by financial circumstances.

Jacquelyn knew that inside the forty rooms, the constant damp air had taken its toll on the interior walls. However, the north wing remained in good repair. It was there that Uncle Luther lived.

Austin parked his car on the graveled drive in front of the north wing. In the silence that followed the switching off of his engine, Jacquelyn could hear the beginning night sounds of the frogs and whippoorwills off in the darkness of the swamp to the south that separated the land of Cypress Halls from Glen Oaks, where Scott McCrann lived.

Scott! The word ripped through Jacquelyn like a jagged sword, slicing her emotions into tattered fragments. In a sudden flash, all the old bitterness and anger bubbled up in her. How stubborn Scott was—and how ruthless! When she had refused to marry him before she'd had a chance to test her wings, he'd resorted to running her brother Gerrard out of business.

It all came back to her in a blinding storm of heated accusations. She had never dreamed that her little bid for independence would unleash such a torrent of evil forces.

She had loved Scott then, or so she had thought. But she had wanted to finish her last year of college. Scott agreed to that. He remained at Glen Oaks while she spent the school year in New Orleans. That summer, after her graduation, Scott had expected her to marry him. But something in her longed for a measure of freedom first. She had spent most of her life at Cypress Halls under the care of Uncle Luther. Now she was being asked to return to the same kind of life, only as Scott McCrann's wife at Glen Oaks. It was what she wanted to do—but not quite yet. Something told her she must have a year to live on her own, to make it as a person in her own right. Maybe it was a need to establish her own identity. Perhaps it was to justify Uncle Luther's confidence in her and to make his sacrifices for her worthwhile.

The family property on which Cypress Halls sat had once been extensive. But through the generations, the family's holdings had dwindled to the mansion proper and a few acres. Uncle Luther had sold off much of the remaining acreage to send Jacquelyn to college and to set Gerrard up in business. How could she accept his help if she never planned to put to use any of the talents she had learned in college? As Scott's wife, there would be no need for her to work. Besides, there was a certain pride in her that begged to be satisfied. It was a pride that said she could make it in the world on her own—not as somebody's wife or as somebody's niece, but as herself. Until that was satisfied, she could not have married Scott.

But Scott became angry with her and didn't understand her needs. They had a bitter quarrel and said many dreadful things to each other, accusations that lingered long after the heat of the argument had died down. Jacquelyn had believed that, in time, she and Scott would patch up their romance. But then Gerrard had come and had told her the awful truth about Scott. She had never been able to feel the same about the man she had once loved after finding out what kind of ruthless person he really was.

The memory of the night Gerrard came to her apartment was bitterly etched in her mind. She'd heard the knock late one night, just as she prepared to go to bed. When she looked through the peephole in her door, she saw a wretched, disheveled Gerrard, and she'd gasped with fright and concern.

She'd opened the door. Gerrard had stumbled in. She saw at once that he had been drinking. He was hatless and coatless, drenched from walking through the rain.

Quickly, she put water on the stove to heat for coffee. She grabbed towels and a robe and got her brother out of his wet shirt. He hunched over the table, his eyes hollow and dark like two burned-out coals.

She had not seen Gerrard in several weeks. Now she was shocked and dismayed at how bad he looked. His cheeks were sunken and feverish. He'd lost a lot of weight. "Gerrard, what on earth is wrong?" she gasped. "Have you been sick?"

He shook his head. "Not the way you think," he mumbled. "It's just that everything's shot. My business, my life—"

"I—I don't understand."

He sighed, shaking his head. He was half incoherent, but as he talked, Jacquelyn began to grasp what had happened. She knew Uncle Luther had given Gerrard money to get started in business. He had opened a lumberyard with the money. Gerrard was her own brother, but she would have been the first to admit that he'd been spoiled by Uncle Luther and Hattie, their nursemaid, when he was a youngster, and he'd been a bit on the wild side as a teenager. Uncle Luther had bailed him out of several scrapes. But the past year he had settled down, she thought, working at making a go of his business. Jacquelyn had thought her brother's future was secure.

But now he was telling her his business was bankrupt. He'd lost everything.

"Oh, Gerrard," she'd wept, her heart going out to her poor brother. She knew how much pride Gerrard had and how humiliating this failure must be. No wonder he was in such a state.

"It's all your ex-boyfriend's fault!" he suddenly cried, the dullness in his eyes giving way to a sudden flaming anger.

"Scott?" Jacquelyn faltered. "I don't understand, Gerrard. How is it his fault?"

"He ran me out of business," Gerrard said bluntly. "You know he has the only other lumberyard in town. He cold-bloodedly set out to destroy me, and he did it. He began cutting prices way below cost.

With his money, he could afford the loss. When I couldn't keep pace, he slashed his prices even deeper. Uncle Luther had no more money to help me. I had to go to the bank to get a loan just to stay in business." A bitter laugh twisted his lips. "You can guess how far I got with the bank. Scott McCrann is on the board of directors, so naturally they turned me down."

Jacquelyn was heartsick. She could see clearly that she was the indirect cause of her brother's tragedy. It was crystal clear to her why Scott had chosen to destroy Gerrard's business so ruthlessly. His precious male ego had been hurt by Jacquelyn's refusal to marry him when he had dictated. Scott McCrann was not accustomed to being turned down by anybody. Smarting under this affront to his male pride, he had chosen to get back at her by cold-bloodedly ruining her brother's life. At that moment, she knew she would despise Scott McCrann to her dying day.

Tearfully, she asked Gerrard what he was going to do. "I don't know," he'd mumbled. "Go someplace else, I guess. Start over. What hurts, Sis, is losing the money Uncle Luther gave me to start my business. The poor old man just doesn't have that kind of money to spare."

Then Jacquelyn thought about Natalie D'Raulde, Austin's beautiful dark-haired sister. She and Gerrard had been sweethearts since childhood and would surely marry one day. "How about Natalie?" Jacquelyn asked.

Gerrard shrugged. "That's over, too. No woman wants a man who's a loser. Everybody said I was too wild and harebrained to ever amount to anything. Ol' Scott saw to it that their predictions came true."

"But you must be wrong about Natalie. She loves

you, Gerrard—has loved you since we were all children together. Surely she'd stick by you. . . ."

Gerrard shrugged. "Don't want her pity. . . ." he mumbled. He stumbled over to the couch and flopped down. He fell into an exhausted sleep. Gently, Jacquelyn had drawn a cover over him, then she'd gone to bed.

When she awoke the next morning, her brother was gone. On the kitchen table was a short note from him:

> Sorry to be such a bother, Sis. You were
> sweet to listen to my troubles. I'm off
> to the West Coast. Maybe my luck will
> change out there.
>
> > Love,
> > Gerrard

A few weeks later she received a letter from him. He'd gotten a job at a lumber camp in Oregon. Since then, they had corresponded from time to time. Gerrard had never been one to write many letters. He seemed to be doing all right in his new career. He was determined to put his old life behind him and never mentioned Natalie in his letters. Apparently she was part of the life he was determined to forget.

With a sigh, she shook off the painful memories, forcing herself back to the present moment.

Darkness had come quite suddenly with a rush of black velvet. Jacquelyn welcomed its comforting arms around her. The house seemed to draw back into a shadowy cloak. At the same time, lights went on behind the shuttered windows of the north wing. Austin lifted Jacquelyn's suitcases out of the trunk, then came around and opened her door. She stepped from the car, painfully and stiffly. The long ride reminded her that she was not entirely free from the aftereffects of her recent ordeal.

From the shadows of the great porch, she heard the sudden growling, snarling charge of one of the biggest and ugliest dogs that had ever drawn a breath.

"Brutus!" Austin said sharply.

Recognizing him, the dog stopped his charge, came up to Austin and sniffed around his legs, his fierce growls turning to greeting whines. But then he moved in Jacquelyn's direction, becoming stiff-legged and suspicious again.

"Good heavens, does Uncle Luther still keep that monster around?" she asked uneasily.

"Oh, he won't hurt you once he remembers you're one of the family." Austin grinned.

"I hope he's got a good memory," Jacquelyn muttered, holding out her hand to him. "Here, Brutus, old fellow. Remember me?"

He indicated by deep-throated growls and showing his teeth that he wasn't sure. But after circling around her a couple of times and sniffing suspiciously, he apparently decided not to tear her limb from limb for the time being. For that she felt grateful.

"Have to keep a watch dog," Austin said. "The house is too tempting a target for prowlers and vandals."

"I'd say Brutus is an excellent choice," Jacquelyn said nervously. "I certainly wouldn't brave his fangs just for a peek inside the house."

They continued up the path and Austin tapped the massive brass knocker at the main door of the north wing. The door opened almost at once, releasing the light behind it. Silhouetted was a familiar figure.

"Hattie!" Jacquelyn exclaimed.

"Miss Jacquelyn! Come in the house, honey. We've been expecting you all afternoon."

Jacquelyn felt a sudden rush of warmth as she gave Hattie a tight hug. Hattie, Uncle Luther's maid, had been a part of the family for as long as Jacquelyn could remember. Jacquelyn hadn't seen Hattie or the house for two years. Only two years, yet it seemed like a lifetime ago. It had been that long ago that she'd left Scott after their bitter argument. With her parents dead, her brother Gerrard moved away and the man she loved turned against her, Jacquelyn had seen no point in ever coming back, except for Uncle Luther's sake. She had moved into an apartment in New Orleans after college and that was where she'd lived ever since.

"We've been so worried since we heard about that terrible accident you were in, Miss Jacquelyn," Hattie exclaimed, looking at her with motherly concern.

"I'm fine now," she reassured Hattie. "I got off lucky. No broken bones or anything like that. But I am still a little sore and stiff."

"Well, it's Jacquelyn," came a deep voice from behind her. She turned to greet Uncle Luther, who was emerging from his study down the hall. Seeing Luther Cordoway was always an experience of some magnitude. His height was impressive—six feet four, to be exact—and he had the shoulders and bones to go with it. More impressive than his towering size, however, was the impact of his forceful personality. It was a bit like being engulfed by the tide.

But as he moved nearer, Jacquelyn saw with a twinge that the last two years had laid a heavy hand on him. His bushy hedge of rusty hair had turned completely white. There was a slight stoop now to his massive shoulders. But his eyes peering at her over his half-moon reading glasses were as sharp as ever.

"Let me look at you, child. Are you sure you're all right?" He scowled.

Jacquelyn had the distinct feeling she was being X-rayed again for broken bones. She felt ashamed that she had allowed herself to be absent so long from the presence of someone who obviously cared so much about her. She forced a laugh. "Positive, Uncle Luther. Just a little sore is all."

"Wretched reckless driver," he muttered. "Ought to be thrown in jail for life. Have the police caught the scoundrel?"

Jacquelyn shook her head. "I doubt that they will."

"Spaced out, no doubt," he grumbled. "Full of drugs, probably. Terrible what the world has come to. Just terrible. But we'll talk about that later. Now, you get yourself settled and then we'll have a nice chat before dinner. Hattie's got the front bedroom all ready for you."

Then he acknowledged Austin with a brief greeting and a request, which was more of an order, to see that her bags got upstairs. Austin led the way, carrying her luggage. Jacquelyn followed, worrying over how deeply she may have hurt Uncle Luther by her long absence. Did he understand why she had not been able to return to Cypress Halls these last two years? While she had never discussed her feelings about Scott with Uncle Luther, the man had a way of reading her soul. He had never urged her to come back against her will until now, when circumstances dictated a rest for her complete recovery. He seemed genuinely happy to see her, not bitter, as she might have supposed. He obviously understood that the reason for her absence had been both deep and personal.

Austin opened the door of the spacious front bedroom, with its elegant canopied bed, exquisite nineteenth-century furniture, handcrafted by New Orleans cabinetmakers over a hundred years ago, and walls freshly papered with a pink rosebud pattern to match the drapes and bedspread. Jacquelyn was surprised at how cozy the room appeared. Its splendor was a sample of how the main section of the house must have looked in its heyday.

"Do you have a room in the north wing, Austin?" Jacquelyn asked. "You wrote that you were living here on the grounds now."

He shook his head. "Uncle Luther had the old plantation overseer's house renovated. I'm staying there. It's not bad, and I'm not far away when he needs me."

A puzzled frown crossed Jacquelyn's brow. Something strange was going on. She knew Uncle Luther was in no financial position to be refurbishing the place. Yet there was clear evidence of recent remodeling.

Austin moved closer, looking at her with dark, brooding eyes. For a moment, they did not speak. Jacquelyn touched his cheek, then he bent and kissed her. In spite of her fervent wish that she could experience some kind of thrill at Austin's advances, Jacquelyn felt nothing.

"It's good to have you home, Jacquelyn," he said huskily.

"Yes, it's good to be here," she whispered, more

in love with this place than she had ever been with Austin. They had shared a thousand childhood experiences in this house, experiences that were memories now, shared by both of them and forming a bond between them. Perhaps there were too many memories going too far back. Perhaps she'd known Austin too well and too long, like a brother, and that had been a barrier as well as a bond.

"Well." He brightened in one of his sudden changes of mood. "I guess I'll get over to my humble abode."

"You're not going to have dinner with us?"

He shook his head. "Not tonight. Uncle Luther wants you all to himself. But I'll be seeing plenty of you while you're here."

"That's a promise?" Jacquelyn asked, hoping to ease some of her feelings of guilt for not caring more deeply for Austin.

"You'd better believe it," he said throatily. His tone made Jacquelyn sorry she had seemed so eager. While she didn't want to encourage Austin unnecessarily, she also didn't want to hurt him. And she knew that no matter how much they saw of each other, she would never feel any more for him.

He kissed her again, lightly this time, and left happily whistling a current popular tune.

Jacquelyn washed her hands in the adjoining bathroom, freshened her makeup and ran a comb through her hair. Then she rejoined Uncle Luther downstairs in his favorite room, the study. He greeted her with a glass of sherry.

"My, but it's a fine sight to have a pretty young woman under this roof again. Just what Cypress Halls has been needing."

"From a practical standpoint, Cypress Halls needs a good deal more than that!" Jacquelyn quipped, beginning to relax with Uncle Luther. "But thank you for the gallant compliment."

Uncle Luther smiled knowingly. "Sit down—sit down, dear," he said in his deep, resonant voice.

Jacquelyn felt a wave of warmth rush over her. Good old Uncle Luther. It was as if she had never left. They were taking up their relationship from where they had left off over two years ago, and it was clear Uncle Luther was not going to question her about her motives for her long absence. Neither was he going to hold it against her.

Gratefully, Jacquelyn took a seat in a comfortable morris chair. The room enveloped her in an aura of comfort and elegance. She'd always suspected that Uncle Luther had spent the small remains of the once considerable Cordoway family wealth in restoring and keeping in good repair this one wing of the old mansion. That was a bit pathetic, like having a handsome captain's quarters in a sinking ship. But, except for Jacquelyn, Uncle Luther was the last of the bloodline of the Cordoways, and the house and grounds and family traditions were the focal point of his life.

This room, except for the modern touches of a window air conditioner and a color television set in one corner, was exactly as it must have been in those prosperous bygone days, with its bronze chandeliers, black Carrara marble mantel with andirons of hammered polished brass, crimson brocade draperies and matching wallpaper. The rosewood furniture, like that in the bedroom upstairs, had been fashioned by the most skilled craftsmen in New Orleans.

On the walls were portraits of some illustrious ancestors, including a famous Civil War general, done in oil by a well-known Philadelphia artist. In a mahogany bookcase imported from France was a collection of rare books of antebellum vintage. It was easy, sitting in this room, to fall under its spell and convince oneself that outside, the Cordoway sugar plantation was in full production, pouring endless streams of gold dollars into the already swollen family coffers, forgetting that that had been more than a hundred years ago.

"Now I want to hear all the details of this misfortune you've had," Uncle Luther said, taking his seat in an easy chair facing Jacquelyn. "All we had were the barest details—that you had been struck by a hit-and-run driver."

"There's not much I can add to what you already know, Uncle Luther," Jacquelyn said. "One night last week I was walking back to my apartment after work. A car went out of control and hit me a glancing blow. When I regained consciousness, I was in a hospital. Nobody got a good look at the car, and of course it was gone by the time the police arrived."

"Shocking," Uncle Luther said, his face grave. "It was a miracle you weren't killed."

"I was lucky." Jacquelyn nodded, a shiver running down her back at the recollection. Then she fished in her dress pocket for the letter she had placed there before coming downstairs. Giving Uncle Luther a sideways glance, she said, "Now, let's talk about this mysterious letter I got from my favorite uncle while I was in the hospital. Beautiful bouquets of flowers every day, a huge basket of fruit, then this letter that has my curiosity working overtime."

Uncle Luther had a sly twinkle in his eye. Obviously, he was enjoying his little mystery to the hilt.

"What's all this secret business about 'the most important commission of my career'?" Jacquelyn asked, eyeing the letter before handing it to Uncle Luther. "Uncle Luther, it was mean of you not to give me more details in the letter," she chided humorously. "I almost tried sneaking out of the hospital two days early, just to get down here and find out what you meant."

He chuckled. Then he leaned back and gazed at her thoughtfully. "Jacquelyn, I've heard through some of my contacts in New Orleans that you have been making quite a name for yourself as an interior decorator. You did over the Lanier mansion in the garden district recently. That old Creole family would never be satisfied with anything but the best."

"You knew about that?" she asked with surprise.

"Oh, I keep in touch with things. Not as buried away down here as you might believe." Then he leaned forward. His face grew flushed and his eyes were suddenly intense. "How would you like to take on something bigger and grander than you've ever dreamed of before—something that would make that Lanier house look like a weekend cottage?" He paused for effect, then delivered his surprise. "How would you like to restore Cypress Halls?"

Jacquelyn stared at him blankly for a moment, wondering if she'd understood correctly. "Restore

Cypress Halls?" she repeated dazedly. "Why, Uncle Luther, it would cost a fortune."

"Yes, it would, but the resources are now at my disposal!"

The news came as a shock to Jacquelyn. She eyed Uncle Luther closely. Was the old man taking leave of his senses?

Chapter Two

Uncle Luther rose and began pacing the room with considerable agitation. "Restoring Cypress Halls has been a lifelong dream of mine, but the cost was always out of the question."

"Yes, I know," Jacquelyn agreed.

"The Cordoways, as you know of course, were once a wealthy family. They came to Louisiana in the 1840s, migrating from the East, and became successful sugarcane planters," Uncle Luther went on as if talking both to her and to some phantom listener who had never heard the family's background before. "They bought a great deal of land, and by the mid-1850s had built this beautiful plantation house, Cypress Halls. They entertained presidents and European royalty. Their children were sent to Paris for an education. It's difficult for us today to visualize the kind of aristocracy and feudal society they lived in. It had its immoral aspects, but its moments of grandeur, too—a flowering of great culture and appreciation of arts and fine manners."

"You love that era, don't you?" Jacquelyn asked.

"Yes. Still, it was destined to pass from the scene. The upheaval of the Civil War, the decline in the cotton and sugarcane markets—these things ended the great plantations. However, unlike many of the plantation families who had to abandon or sell their big houses, the Cordoways somehow managed to hold onto Cypress Halls through successive generations. They had owned a great deal of land, and by selling that off a little at a time and having mild successes in other ventures, my grandfather and father were able to keep a fraction of the original family fortune. But there was never enough to keep the big house up, and it gradually went downhill. By the time the place fell into my hands, I had to settle for keeping this one wing livable."

He paused for a sip of sherry, then continued, waving his cigar for emphasis. "I've spent my life trying to regain some of the Cordoway prestige and wealth. But financial success has eluded me, Jacquelyn. It's been like a tantalizing phantom, teasing me in many guises, but always evading my grasp at the last moment. Finally, after a lot of deep reflection, I realized that I was never destined to achieve my life's goal through my own efforts. I had to turn to somebody else for the solution. It was when I had almost given up hope that I was handed an opportunity to achieve my dream of restoring the mansion."

"What happened, Uncle Luther?" Jacquelyn asked, curiosity making her tingle all over.

"I've been offered a deal," Uncle Luther said, his eyes sparkling with a mixture of excitement and a hint of despair. "An interested party has agreed to buy the mansion and property, with the stipulation that I can live here the rest of my life as the proprietor of the house. Everything will be under my control, just as it is now. But on my death, the entire estate will revert to the buyer. In exchange for this agreement, the new owner will furnish the funds for a total restoration of Cypress Halls. And Jacquelyn, I want you to do the refurbishing."

Jacquelyn suddenly felt her mouth go dry. This was astounding news. She didn't know what to say or exactly how she felt about it. She recognized a growing anger that fate had played such a cruel trick on Uncle Luther. He could realize his lifelong dream to restore Cypress Halls only at the expense of deeding it after his death into the hands of a stranger. What kind of a hideous joke was that?

"This affects your future, too, Jacquelyn," Uncle Luther went on, eyeing her closely. "If I had hung on to Cypress Halls, it would have been yours and Gerrard's some day. I know he has never cared for the place in the same way you have. I did everything in my power to preserve the mansion for you. But the matter has been taken out of my hands. The place is deteriorating badly. If it's not restored soon, there will be nothing of any value left to leave you. I had a hard choice to make, Jacquelyn. Sell, and see our family home rise from its foundations to its former splendor, or keep it, and watch it waste away into certain ruin."

A sudden pang shot through Jacquelyn. While she had left here two years ago not knowing if she would ever return, she had always harbored in the back of her mind a certain sense that this rambling structure was her home, a place where she had put down roots and could always return if she felt the need. But now, Uncle Luther was telling her that someday Cypress Halls would fall into the hands of a new owner and she would have no further claim on the place.

Jacquelyn sat stunned, her mind still reeling from Uncle Luther's revelation. It was something she was going to have to think about. It took time to digest a concept that struck at the very foundations of a basic belief she had held but had never really thought much about before. She had always assumed Cypress Halls would be open to her any time she needed it. She had just taken it for granted.

Uncle Luther paused for a moment. He looked directly at Jacquelyn. She saw him studying her puzzled expression.

"Stored away in trunks are all the original plans, specifications and descriptions of the house and its furnishings when it was new," Uncle Luther offered, as if prompting her to agree to help him. "You can use that information as a guide. With your training and talent in interior decorating, you can do an excellent job. Whatever it costs, I want you to restore Cypress Halls to its original magnificence."

"Oh, Uncle Luther!" Jacquelyn cried, her large blue eyes sparkling with excitement overshadowed by dismay. "Me? Restore Cypress Halls? I—I don't know how to respond. It's a dream job. But to redecorate it for somebody else, I don't know . . ."

"Say yes, Jacquelyn," Uncle Luther urged. "We are living in an ugly, barbaric age of utilitarian concrete and plastic, an age when good manners and morals have gone out of the world. I believe it is important to preserve these symbols of the past with their great charm and elegance.

"It is fashionable these days to think we must have a homogeneous society in which each person is a dreary equal of his peer. Bah! Equality is a myth, Jacquelyn. Some of us are smarter than others, some more productive. The individual is what is important —what he can achieve in open competition with others. I don't believe in a classless society. Equal opportunity, yes, but guaranteed equality, never. Therefore I want this proud old house to stand as a link with an age when men dared to be proud and aristocratic."

Uncle Luther was breathing hard. His face was flushed. He seemed a little mad. But his obsession was contagious. The thought of transforming those ruined halls to their original grandeur, of restoring or duplicating the work of the original craftsmen, was intoxicating.

"Well, what do you say, Jacquelyn?" He was standing before her, his shaggy head bent forward eagerly, his fierce brows looking like wild hedges, his eyes blazing feverishly.

"I—I really don't know, Uncle Luther," Jacquelyn confessed. "You've floored me with all this so suddenly. Please let me have a little while to get used to the idea. I'll admit I'm tempted."

"Of course." He patted her hand. "I didn't mean to high-pressure you the minute you arrived. Come now, Hattie is ready to serve dinner. She's cooked some of her best Creole dishes especially for you."

Uncle Luther gallantly escorted Jacquelyn to the dining room. She smiled, chatting aimlessly about life in New Orleans, trying to cover the concern in her voice.

The prospect of restoring Cypress Halls to its former elegance thrilled her beyond comprehension.

It was a project any interior decorator would give half her life for. But Jacquelyn was not an ordinary decorator. She had lived much of her life within these walls . . . and near Scott McCrann, after he had taken possession of the neighboring estate. How could she give Uncle Luther an answer until she'd had time to sort through her own feelings? There were so many things to consider. Could she cope with the possibility of seeing Scott from time to time? Could she handle the pain of restoring the mansion for someone else? In her still weakened state from her accident, she couldn't make a decision like that now.

Hattie's dinner, which consisted of turtle soup, a main dish of baked eggplant with shrimp and crabmeat, a dessert of crêpes suzette, everything ending on the proper final note with café brûlot, was equal to anything the best chefs at Antoine's or Galatorie's could have prepared. After the hospital fare Jacquelyn had been having the past week, every morsel was pure rapture.

But Jacquelyn's mind continuously strayed from the delicious meal to Uncle Luther's surprising news. The possibility of restoring Cypress Halls was staggering. She, too, was emotionally involved with this old house. She had grown up in the shadow of its legends, played in its deserted galleries, listened at night for ghosts. The Cordoway blood coursed through her veins, too, and as long as this old house stood, it would be a symbolic factor in her psychological makeup. Not to help restore it would be to deny a part of her own identity.

Still, there was Scott McCrann to consider. And it was because of him that she had moved away in the first place.

On the other hand, what an opportune excuse for staying away from New Orleans for a while! Jacquelyn had to admit to a disquieting uneasiness in the city. The French Quarter had provided her with a link to the Old World atmosphere she had grown up with and had come to love. But still, she was living in the city, and shopping trips into the modern areas of town and clients in the affluent garden district were daily reminders that her apartment in the Old World part of town was merely an enclave surrounded by the plastic and concrete Uncle Luther had so severely criticized. She had to admit she agreed with him.

Later that night, Jacquelyn lay on the big canopied bed, too agitated to sleep. From an open window came the perfume of magnolia blossoms and the song of a night bird. On an impulse, she put on slippers and a robe and picked up a flashlight she'd found on the dresser. She went downstairs and quietly let herself out a side door. The full moon had risen above the moss-draped cypress trees at the rim of the swamp and had coated the ruins of Cypress Halls with a silvery patina.

Brutus came snarling out of the darkness. "It's only me, you ugly monster," she said, trying not to sound nervous. She'd read somewhere that the scent of human fear enraged mean dogs.

Either she fooled him, or somewhere in the instincts of his murky, vicious brain he had accepted the fact that she belonged there. He sniffed around her for a bit, then slunk off into the darkness again.

Jacquelyn moved around back of the house to the garden. This vast formal garden covering several acres had once been as much of a showplace as the house itself. She could see that Uncle Luther had already begun restoration here in the garden. The tangled undergrowth had been cleared away. The hedges that bordered the graveled paths had been trimmed. The winding paths took her past lush semitropical growths of palmettoes and Spanish dagger, flowering oleanders and crêpe myrtle, the magnolias, azaleas, camellias and lilies.

A series of terraces led down to a sunken rose garden. Here was the garden's marble statuary, looking like pale ghosts in the shadows. The life-size classical figures were also casualties of time. Venus had been decapitated. The discus thrower lacked an arm. Time and rain had mottled the marble. Some of the statues were almost totally cloaked with vines.

Beyond this edge of the garden, under a spread of great oaks, was Uncle Luther's carefully tended roque court. Along with his record library of classical music, the game of roque was Uncle Luther's great passion in life. A very distant cousin of lawn croquet, roque, played the way Uncle Luther played it, became a vicious challenge of skill and psychology. Jacquelyn could, with very little imagination, hear those hard rubber balls caroming off the steel banks with the lethal "smack!" of a ricocheting bullet.

Jacquelyn sat on a stone bench and gazed through the leafy fringes of banana leaves at the outlines of the big house. In that nostalgic setting, childhood memories assailed her. There had been four of them: her brother Gerrard, Jacquelyn, and Austin D'Raulde and his beautiful sister, Natalie. They had been inseparable when they were children. They had played marvelous games of hide-and-seek here in the tangled jungle of the old garden, and they had ventured into the edges of the swamp in search of

Jean Laffitte's buried treasure that everyone on the bayou knew for certain had to be around here someplace.

But the big house had been the real storybook setting for their childish imaginations. They had spent many rainy days on its galleries and exploring the large rooms. The jagged wound left by the Civil War cannonball that had crashed through the ballroom had been material for a hundred imaginary childhood dreams. Gerrard and Austin fought endless duels with willow stick rapiers under the oaks, where, according to Uncle Luther, many real duels had been fought a century ago.

Natalie, with her vivid imagination, had made up the plots of most of the stories the children had acted out. It was she who had gotten the idea that somewhere hidden in the walls of the mansion was a lost map of the Laffitte treasure, and the search for it had gone on all through their childhood.

It was Natalie who had seen the ghost of Cypress Halls and had talked the others into some bone-chilling night watches to try to catch sight of it. In their childish fantasies, they had heard plenty of sounds—footsteps, creaking doors, sighs—but only Natalie claimed to have seen the ghostly wraith one night, descending the great spiral stairway. Had it been only a joke, had she been lying for the sheer fun of it, or had the girl really imagined she saw the specter that occupied so many of their games?

Natalie, whose beauty as a child had been almost unreal! Her hair and eyes were jet black and her skin was as delicate and translucent as the finest, most fragile china. She had an aristocratic nose, a proud tilt to her chin, and sensual lips. As children, Natalie and Jacquelyn had been as close as sisters, loving each other with a deep bond of affection. But when they reached adolescence, an underlying rivalry sprang up between them. It hurt her to see her relationship with her closest friend marred. Why had they grown apart? Had it been some kind of basic female conflict? Was Natalie jealous of Jacquelyn's position in Uncle Luther's household and her claim on Cypress Halls? Or, Jacquelyn asked her own heart with a blush of shame, had the fault been her own—some kind of unconscious teenage jealousy over Natalie's beauty?

Jacquelyn's thoughts were drawn further into the past. Memories crowded her reverie like turning pages of a yellowed scrapbook. Natalie and her brother, Austin, came from a proud old Creole family that dated back to the first French settlers. But their family plantation house had burned to the ground in the Civil War, and the last few remaining acres of their once vast lands had been sold or mortgaged by their father. They had lived in a modest frame house on the bayou. Their father did some trading and shipping, though he depended mostly on the charity of relatives in New Orleans who were somewhat better off.

There was rumored to be a streak of insanity in their family. How true that was, Jacquelyn wasn't sure, but she did know their mother had had an incurable mental breakdown and had died in a state institution for the insane. Mr. D'Raulde completed his job of drinking himself to death a few years later. Then Uncle Luther, who had been close to the family, saw that Austin and Natalie were properly raised by Luther's widowed sister-in-law, Perforce.

Austin and Jacquelyn had always been close. But Natalie was jealous of the fact that Jacquelyn and

Gerrard were not as poor as she and Austin were. Jacquelyn's mother, who was Uncle Luther's sister, had married Gus La Salle, a jolly, easygoing Acadian. He operated a store in the bayou settlement near Cypress Halls. Gerrard and Jacquelyn were born in their neat white frame cottage.

It was when Jacquelyn was six and her brother eight that her parents were killed in a fire that burned their home to the ground. Both children might have perished in that fire, too, but they had been spending the week at Uncle Luther's home, as they often did. From that time on, they remained at Cypress Halls and were raised by Uncle Luther and Hattie.

As they grew up, Uncle Luther, openly dubious about the efficacy of public school education, made certain they became familiar with his library of books and records. Under the great columns of the neglected mansion, Jacquelyn made lasting friendships with the characters between the covers of *Pride and Prejudice, Vanity Fair, Ivanhoe, Tom Sawyer, David Copperfield, Treasure Island* and many others. By the time she was in high school, she had progressed to Chaucer, Shakespeare, Goethe, and Thoreau.

Jacquelyn and Gerrard once made bets as to who could read *Jane Eyre* by candlelight inside one of the deserted rooms of the main section of Cypress Halls at midnight. Gerrard won. It had been an interesting childhood.

The children had paired off in natural fashion. Jacquelyn was Austin's girl, and Gerrard and Natalie were childhood sweethearts. When they were grown, they would have a double wedding and go right on living here on the bayou in the shadow of Cypress Halls for the rest of their days.

But their childhood dreams had met a different fate. Gerrard was destined to leave Natalie, bitter and disillusioned, to seek a new life far away. And as for Austin and Jacquelyn, Scott McCrann was destined to come between them.

Scott had come into her life when she was still in high school. His father, who had considerable capital, had bought into the shrimping business in the area, acquiring a fleet of shrimp boats. He also bought Glen Oaks, a neighboring antebellum mansion, and had it completely renovated.

Jacquelyn was to discover an overwhelming love in Scott's arms. But a bitter quarrel had torn them apart. Then Scott had revealed his ruthless streak. His masculine pride wounded, demanding revenge, he had struck back at her by cruelly running her brother out of business. She had hated Scott ever since.

Jacquelyn sighed and told herself it was pointless to start thinking about the past. She arose from the garden bench and started back to the north wing of the house. On her way, she again encountered Brutus, who sniffed menacingly in her direction and bared his teeth silently but let her pass. She went quietly to her room and took a sleeping pill.

The next morning, with daylight streaming through her window and the sound of voices downstairs, the gloom and depression of the night before abated somewhat.

Jacquelyn dressed in a sundress with a flared skirt. September could be muggy and warm, and she hated the heat. She slipped into a pair of thin-strapped sandals with a small heel. Her stiff joints were loosening up, and the bruises were slowly fading. She felt almost normal, except for an ache in her heart for a past gone forever and a future that was never to be.

Downstairs, Jacquelyn found Uncle Luther and Austin having breakfast on the terrace.

"Good morning," she said, smiling.

"Good morning," Austin said, rising and pulling out a chair for her. His dark eyes roved over her approvingly. It flattered her when a man looked at her like that, but only one man could send a lightning bolt through her with his glance, and he was a man she had learned to hate.

"I was hoping you would come down in time to join us," Uncle Luther said, rising and bending slightly from the waist in a small, courtly bow.

"You should have had Hattie call me," Jacquelyn apologized. "I'm not usually this lazy."

"Oh, you need the rest," Uncle Luther said. "Anyway, you're dressed now and in plenty of time for some of Hattie's delicious strawberry pancakes."

"I have to drive over to LaMere after breakfast, Jacquelyn," Austin said. "Would you like to go along for the ride?"

"I'd love to," Jacquelyn said. "Perhaps I can see Aunt Perforce while we are there."

Austin smiled over his cup of coffee and nodded.

Jacquelyn found her appetite whetted again by Hattie's great cooking and she devoured a stack of pancakes and a glass of milk.

She and Uncle Luther chatted casually with Austin, and she realized Uncle Luther was pointedly not pressing her about a decision on remodeling Cypress Halls. For that she was grateful. She still hadn't made up her mind, and last night's reminiscing out in the garden only served to confuse her more about what she should do. Perhaps she should decline Uncle Luther's offer and return to New Orleans immediately, before she had the misfortune to run into Scott. At least now, before she saw him in person again, she had a semblance of her wits about her.

Thirty minutes later, Jacquelyn and Austin were in the car on the way to the little bayou settlement, LaMere, the nearest community to Cypress Halls.

"Did you know Uncle Luther has invited a crowd over on Friday for a jambalaya?" Austin asked as they drove along a narrow road atop a levee flanking a bayou.

"No. He hadn't told me."

"Yes, a kind of family gathering, I suppose you would say, to welcome you home. Everyone will be there."

Austin took his eyes from the road and looked directly at her as he had said "everyone." Apprehension streaked through Jacquelyn. "Everyone" would include his sister, Natalie and . . . Scott McCrann. If Austin was judging her reaction, she wondered if the sudden rush of warmth to her cheeks was very noticeable.

Jacquelyn became quiet and introspective on the twenty-minute ride to LaMere. The small cluster of frame buildings included a general store, a filling station, a post office, a marine repair shop and a dance hall. She commented, "It hasn't changed much."

"No reason why it should," Austin replied. "Not much else is needed by the people who live here along the bayou. They trap the nutria, catch the crayfish, get to the dance hall on Saturday night and the little Catholic church on Sunday morning, same as their ancestors have done for the past hundred years or so."

"It's a way of life—not a bad one, I suspect."

"There are worse these days," Austin agreed. "I have to go to the post office, then pick up some things for Uncle Luther at the general store. Do you want to go with me or stop off to see Aunt Perforce?"

"Oh, I'd really like to see her, Austin. Do you mind?"

"Of course not," Austin said with a touch of disappointment. In spite of the fact that Austin had known for some time that Jacquelyn didn't love him, he seemed never to give up hope that she would someday change her mind.

He pulled up before a small frame house enclosed by a white picket fence. He reached over and their fingers entwined. "I'll be back in a little while."

She squeezed his hand fondly. Although she didn't love him in a romantic way, she felt strongly that special closeness they shared. If Scott hadn't come along when he did, Jacquelyn would probably never have known that true love can shake one to her foundations and take one's breath away. Most likely, she would have accepted her relationship with Austin as logically leading to the altar and would be married to him now. If that had happened, life certainly would be much simpler.

Austin reached over and opened the door for her. She stepped out, entered Aunt Perforce's front yard through the gate and went up to her front door and knocked.

"Jacquelyn La Salle!" came the high-pitched

voice. "Well, I heard you were back at your Uncle Luther's for a visit. Come in, child, come in."

Aunt Perforce, like the town of LaMere, had changed little. She was as tall and strong as ever, and her glittering black eyes were, if anything, more piercing. Her home had become more cluttered, if that was possible. Aunt Perforce never threw anything away. Consequently, every table and chair was piled high with old newspapers and magazines. Astrology was Aunt Perforce's ruling passion in life. Books on the subject filled many shelves.

She moved an armful of newspapers from a chair so Jacquelyn could sit. Then she insisted on brewing a cup of alfalfa tea, which she said would be of therapeutic value during Jacquelyn's convalescence.

"They told me about the terrible accident you had." Aunt Perforce clucked her tongue. "You must be very careful for the next several weeks, Jacquelyn. Your stars are in a critical position. There could be much danger for you."

Jacquelyn listened to Aunt Perforce with a tolerant inward smile. She forced herself to swallow some of the noxious-tasting concoction her aunt had brewed and looked around at the familiar dusty, cluttered room. How often she had played here with Austin and Natalie! After their mother had been committed to the state institution and their father had died, they had been raised by Aunt Perforce, a distant relative, with Uncle Luther's financial help.

"How long will you be staying at Cypress Halls, Jacquelyn?" she asked. She arranged herself comfortably in a rocking chair with her cup of tea, which she sipped with unexplained relish.

"It could be for a while," Jacquelyn admitted. "Uncle Luther has asked me to help him restore

Cypress Halls." While she still hadn't decided whether to accept Uncle Luther's offer, Jacquelyn found this a good time to give the prospect a try and see how she felt about it. By admitting the possibility to Aunt Perforce, she was trying it on for size. She rather liked the feel of it.

"He's quite insane, you know," Aunt Perforce said matter-of-factly, as if the fact were common knowledge. "But he's a Scorpio and they tend to get that way—domineering, ordering everyone about. He made up his mind as a young man he was going to rebuild that old monstrosity, and the devil himself couldn't stand in his way." Aunt Perforce crossed herself.

Had it been anyone else speaking, Jacquelyn would have taken offense at such an outrageous remark. But she was accustomed to Aunt Perforce's rantings about Uncle Luther and so just smiled indulgently.

"It's been a lifelong dream of his," Jacquelyn said, "and now he can afford to do it."

"Yes, I know all about the deal he made," Aunt Perforce said. "And I also know Luther has plans for you to refurbish the old place. So you'll be back here, and, of course, you'll see Scott McCrann again. And there will be trouble between you and Natalie."

Jacquelyn felt a stinging rush of warmth to her cheeks. Aunt Perforce could be painfully blunt, and blamed that characteristic on having been born under the sign of Sagittarius.

"What do you mean, there will be trouble between Natalie and me?"

"When your brother Gerrard left, Natalie was

heartbroken. You know they'd been childhood sweethearts. But then, perhaps on the rebound, she began seeing Scott McCrann. I understand they're having quite a love affair."

Jacquelyn almost strangled on the words that she forced herself to utter. "What's that to me? I have no interest in Scott anymore."

"My dear, you may fool yourself, but you can't fool me," Aunt Perforce said confidently. "Don't you think I've spent enough time casting all of your horoscopes? You and Scott were meant for each other. But there is destined to be a great deal of conflict in your relationship before you can work out the differences that divide you."

"We'll never work out our differences," Jacquelyn said coolly. "It's too late for that. The chasm is too wide."

"Don't be too sure," Aunt Perforce corrected her. "Why do you think you came back here? I'll tell you. Because strong forces arranged it. You must be careful in your dealings with Natalie and Scott. Fortunately, you are a Capricorn and the Saturn influence makes you reserved and thoughtful and quite capable in practical matters. But you Capricorns are also capricious when it comes to emotional matters, and that is where trouble could lie. . . ."

"Don't worry, Aunt Perforce," Jacquelyn said. "I don't plan to see much of Scott. I won't have any reason to. What was between us is over. Dead. Forever."

"Don't be fooled, Jacquelyn," Aunt Perforce said knowingly. "You can't refurbish Cypress Halls without encountering Scott almost daily. He'll expect you to consult with him regularly, you know."

"About what?" Jacquelyn asked, bewildered by Aunt Perforce's apparent inside knowledge of something Jacquelyn obviously was not privy to.

"About the decorating. After all, the deal Uncle Luther agreed to for the restoration of the mansion was made with Scott McCrann."

Chapter Three

Jacquelyn stumbled down the road as best she could, trying to see through the mist of tears blurring her vision.

It was all too awful. The one person in all the world who she hated most, Scott McCrann, was the new owner of Cypress Halls! And Uncle Luther wanted her to redecorate the mansion, which would eventually fall into the hands of the man who had broken her heart and had ruthlessly run her brother, Gerrard, out of business for revenge.

How could Uncle Luther have been so cruel to put her in such a position? She had always thought he loved her. Surely he must have believed that she no longer had any feelings left for Scott, not even hate. Otherwise, he would never have asked her to subject herself to Scott's presence, knowing that they had been so much in love at one time. How quickly that love had turned to hate!

After Aunt Perforce's startling revelation, Jacquelyn had no longer been able to concentrate on their conversation. She had fibbed that she had promised to meet Austin at the store and had left, preferring to walk the three blocks rather than listen to any more comments from Aunt Perforce about Scott.

Jacquelyn was glad for the cool sundress she had chosen to wear on this balmy day. Emotional upsets always made her feel flushed. She blinked her eyes against the glare of the sun and brushed a tear from her cheek. Her sandals crunched over the shell road, the sound echoing relentlessly in her ears.

As she approached the post office, she saw a tall, rangy figure with unruly light brown hair leaving the building. He stopped. Their eyes met. Jacquelyn's heart gave a sudden lurch. Then anger bubbled up in her.

"Hello, Jacquelyn," said Scott McCrann.

Jacquelyn felt the life draining out of her. Her knees shook, her mouth turned dry. An electric shock wave shot through her. So this was what it felt like, seeing Scott again. She had wondered many times how she would react, had replayed the scene over in her imagination thousands of times. But it hit her harder than she had ever expected.

Scott moved closer. His tall, lanky figure, his shock of wild brown hair, his intense blue eyes rimmed with a thin band of gray around the irises were exactly as she had remembered in a hundred dreams. But there was a difference about him, too. He seemed older than his thirty-four years. Were there sudden shadows in his eyes, shadows that reflected worry or unhappiness? Or was she imagining it?

For an instant, all the tingling excitement of first feeling in love arrested Jacquelyn's emotions. Then the hatred broke through the surface and she stiffened.

Inadvertently, their hands met, and, in spite of herself, Jacquelyn felt the same well-remembered thrill of physical awareness. Time had not dulled his effect on her as much as she had hoped. His strong, tanned fingers squeezed hers in a welcoming touch. Selfishly, she wanted more than that—to feel his arms pulling her close—but then she remembered what a ruthless individual he was, and her heart turned to ice.

For a second, Jacquelyn thought she saw an expression of softness on Scott's face. But then his features turned cold.

"Everyone has been worried about you, Jacquelyn," he said stiffly, releasing her hand.

Did "everyone" include Scott? Had he been worried about her, too? Was there genuine concern for her in his eyes? Did he still care for her?

No, that was impossible, Jacquelyn thought miserably. There had been too many harsh words between them, hurts that went too deep and were too bitter to ever heal.

A multitude of hurting memories were crowding her mind: Scott's warm lips pressing against hers in their first earthshaking kiss; Scott's golden tanned body on the beach that summer beside hers; that feeling of suffocating awareness as his gaze roamed over her scantily beach-clad figure; the shivery touch of his fingers rubbing suntan lotion on her bare shoulders.

Surely Scott must be remembering, too! Jacquelyn flushed at the thought. She could tell by the narrowing of Scott's eyes that he mistook her embarrassment for anger. It was natural that he would suppose she would react to him with hostility.

Then Austin drove up. Jacquelyn's heart screamed "No." She wanted a few more moments with Scott before all the old anger returned. Just a few stolen minutes for a forbidden affair of the heart, for that's all it could ever be with Scott. It was too late for anything more.

The two men greeted each other. Austin gave Jacquelyn a searching look, trying to decide, she supposed, how she was reacting to seeing Scott.

Austin's presence brought reality crashing in on Jacquelyn again, and she marveled that she could have allowed herself, even for a moment, to feel any of the old tingle that Scott had once created in her. It was just the suddenness of seeing him so unexpectedly, she assured herself. There was certainly no love left between them.

"I drove to Aunt Perforce's to pick you up," Austin said. "She said you had started down here on foot." He eyed her quizzically.

"Yes, Aunt Perforce was horoscoping me to death," Jacquelyn explained.

The three of them stood silent for what seemed an eon. Finally, Austin spoke up. "Are you ready?" he asked her, motioning toward the car.

"Yes," Jacquelyn replied, flashing Scott a disdainful glance.

Austin took her arm and helped direct her toward the car. "Well," he said to Scott in parting, "I guess we'll be seeing you tomorrow at Uncle Luther's get-together?"

"Yes, we'll be there," Scott murmured.

Did Jacquelyn detect a peculiar emphasis on the word *we?* Or was it just her imagination? She knew very well, from what Aunt Perforce had told her, that Scott's date would be Natalie. So what! she thought belligerently. It didn't matter one bit to her whom Scott dated. She had no claim on him anymore and didn't want any.

On the way back to Cypress Halls, Austin drove silently, leaving Jacquelyn alone with her thoughts. She tried to distract her mind with the scenery, with plans on how best to restore Cypress Halls, anything to escape the memories of Scott McCrann. But those memories persisted.

Jacquelyn had developed a mad crush on Scott from the start. But in spite of her intense feeling, considerable time had elapsed before a real romance had developed. She daydreamed about him, worshipped him from a distance when he came to Uncle Luther's home to discuss business. He was cordial to her, but always distant. She later found out that he, too, had been attracted to her from the start, but had thought her too young for him. His defense was to keep his emotional distance.

Then Scott spent several years away from home on business ventures, building his family's fortune. By then his father had died and Scott had taken over the McCrann interests. When he returned to Glen Oaks, Jacquelyn had grown into a young woman.

That summer, their romance bloomed—all tenderness and passion blended into a sweeping intensity. Jacquelyn thought nothing could come between them. She had been destined all her life to belong to Scott McCrann. It almost convinced her that Aunt Perforce was right—the stars had brought their lives together. But if that were true, they had also been fated to part.

The trouble between them began when Jacquelyn insisted on completing her college degree. Scott, accustomed to taking charge of matters, urged her to drop out of school and marry him at once. What was the point of her having a college degree? He could certainly afford to take care of her, and planned to do so. But she showed her own stubborn streak and stood her ground.

It was their first angry quarrel. Scott said she was being unreasonable and stubborn. She accused him of being dictatorial. Finally, love won out. Scott tempered his demands. They patched things up and she went on to finish school. But then their differences flared anew. Scott had visited her frequently during her school year in New Orleans. They had carefully avoided talking about their misunderstanding over her motivation to finish school. She realized now that that had been a fatal mistake. She had never been able to make Scott understand the need she had to establish herself as an independent individual before becoming his wife. When she broke the news to him that she intended to work at her profession as an interior decorator for at least a year before settling down to marriage, it had been the last straw. Scott had stormed out, saying she'd made her choice between a career and him.

Even that quarrel might have been patched up. But when Jacquelyn discovered what Scott had done to her brother, the intense love she had once felt turned into a fury that consumed the tenderness she had once felt for him. The memory of their physical attraction still lingered, but that was all.

Austin pulled up at Cypress Halls, and Jacquelyn

was grateful to be back. "See you later," she said, hopping out of the car.

After lunch, Uncle Luther took Jacquelyn over to the main wing of the house to discuss plans for the renovation.

"Well, Jacquelyn," Uncle Luther said at last. "Have you made up your mind? Will you stay and redecorate Cypress Halls?"

Until that moment, Jacquelyn couldn't have said for sure what her decision would be. She felt very obligated to Uncle Luther. Yet she dreaded having to deal with Scott, who was heartlessly taking her uncle's home from him indirectly.

Uncle Luther couldn't possibly know what he was asking of her. He couldn't know the aching pain she felt. He had no way of guessing how much hurt she was bound to endure in the company of Scott McCrann. And she couldn't tell him. It was a matter too private and too close to her deepest emotions, to discuss how her tender young love had been twisted and turned into hate by exposure to the evil ruthlessness of the man to whom she had once given her heart.

And yet, as Jacquelyn looked at Uncle Luther peering at her over his half-moon reading glasses, she saw a glimmer in his eyes reflecting the same kind of intense pain she herself had felt when she and Scott had learned to hate each other. It was like a lightning bolt hitting her! How selfish she would be to refuse. It was partly because of her that Uncle Luther was in this position. In her young mind, she had not realized the sacrifice her uncle had made for her by selling off the remaining acreage of Cypress Halls to send her to school. He had sacrificed what he loved to give her a chance at what she wanted in life. He had done it unselfishly, never asking for anything in return. And now, when he needed her help, how could she put her own feelings first?

This was Jacquelyn's opportunity to give Uncle Luther what he wanted most in life—Cypress Halls restored to mint condition. And by supervising the redecorating, she would be putting her family's stamp on the mansion to carry the Cordoway touch on into the future, in spite of the fact that the estate would fall into someone else's ownership. It was more than a job Uncle Luther was asking her to do. It was a labor of love. It was only love stronger than her hate of Scott that could keep her here.

"Yes," she said softly. "I'm going to stay."

"That's my girl," Uncle Luther said huskily, taking her hands in his massive ones and patting them kindly. "I've missed you. It will be wonderful having you here again, and I know that only you, who has a real feeling for this old place, could restore it in the proper fashion."

"It's going to be a real challenge," Jacquelyn admitted.

"And one you will meet with your usual high degree of success," Uncle Luther replied confidently.

"I hope so, Uncle Luther," Jacquelyn replied, her nerve ends tingling with excitement at the prospect. It would be a marvelous opportunity for her. Her deep love for Cypress Halls could find a visual expression through her decorating abilities. And with the carte blanche Uncle Luther was offering her and an apparently endless bank account, Jacquelyn could select the very finest of everything. She could hardly wait to get started.

But Uncle Luther had other plans before Jacquelyn could actually begin any real work. He wanted his niece to spend a few more days recuperating, and he had planned a couple of parties for her benefit. She knew at least one of those parties included Scott and Natalie.

"Roque," Uncle Luther said to her, "like chess, is a game that not only tests the skill, but also probes the psychology of the contestants."

It was the afternoon of the following day. Uncle Luther's guests were assembled under the moss-draped limbs of the giant oaks around his roque courts. Nearby, a long picnic table was loaded down with Hattie's crawfish gumbo along with other spicy bayou dishes. The guests had begun arriving at three o'clock. Among the neighbors and friends Uncle Luther had invited—some from as far away as New Orleans—were Ed Jarmon, Uncle Luther's lawyer, and his wife, and Uncle Luther's physician, Dr. Dave Chauvin, and his wife. Aunt Perforce was present; as were Scott and Natalie.

Jacquelyn's first response on seeing Natalie was to eye her closely. Just how close had she and Scott become? How possessive did Scott act around Natalie? Did Natalie respond to Scott like a woman in love? She could not be sure, Jacquelyn thought miserably.

Natalie's wild, dark beauty was still as intense as Jacquelyn remembered. Her black eyes sparkled with the high mirth of a triumphant woman. A feeling stirred in Jacquelyn. Was it a reawakening of the jealousy Jacquelyn felt so ashamed of? Jacquelyn wondered whether the smile on Natalie's face reflected a true inner happiness or whether she was smirking over having won Scott.

Scott, on the other hand, looked almost angry. He shot Jacquelyn a withering glance, mumbled a perfunctory hello to her and lost himself on the other side of the yard.

Finally, Uncle Luther called for a game of roque, and the contestants squared off on the playing field.

The roque court, thirty feet by sixty feet, bore some resemblance to croquet. But the wickets were made of steel and were set rigidly in concrete foundations. The playing surface was smooth, hard-packed sand rather than grass, and the boundaries were concrete curbing that surrounded the court. Unlike simple lawn croquet, roque challenged the skill of the players in banking their hard rubber balls off the curbs.

Jacquelyn's upbringing at Cypress Halls had included a thorough schooling in the fine points of the game. She knew, for example, that the wickets were made of 5/8-inch steel and the hard rubber balls were 3 1/8 inches in diameter. As in serious croquet matches, no self-respecting roque player would enter a game without his own personal custom-made mallet. Uncle Luther's mallet, which he kept in a glass case on the wall of his study between games, had been ordered by Abercrombie and Fitch from John Jaques and Son, Ltd., in England. It was a highly polished, formidable piece made of lignum vitae with a smooth face of laminated plastic on one end and rubber on the other.

Uncle Luther had just finished a series of aggressive plays and had walked over to the bench where Jacquelyn was sitting. He was breathing hard and his face looked pinched. He slipped a pill under his tongue as he sat down.

Consternation furrowed Jacquelyn's brow. "Are you all right, Uncle Luther?" she asked, concerned.

"Yes, yes," he replied impatiently. "Just old age." The color was returning to his face, and his breathing grew easier. He brushed aside any further questions about his health and talked about the game. After his statement about how the game revealed the psychology of the players, he went on to say, "You can learn a lot about a man by watching him play." He motioned in the direction of the court.

Scott was standing over a ball, his mallet poised. His tall, lean frame was hunched over slightly as he eyed the ball, just ready to smack it. He was the picture of intense concentration, a jungle cat poised to spring.

Jacquelyn couldn't keep her gaze from straying to the ripple of his thigh muscles under his tight trousers, his lean hips and the broad shoulders that strained against his white shirt. She might hate the man, but her physical desire could still be aroused by the sight of his magnificent body, she thought with a shameful blush.

"You take Scott, there," Uncle Luther continued. "He plays a hard, serious game. A little bit on the ruthless side." The old man chuckled. "Maybe that's why I like to play against him. Doctor Chauvin cheats. Have to keep an eye on him all the time or he will nudge a ball when no one is watching to gain a better position. Austin is only a medium to fair player—doesn't have enough of the killer instinct. But he's patient and has a good eye and occasionally pulls off some brilliant long shots."

Jacquelyn listened politely, but she didn't particularly enjoy these roque games of Uncle Luther's.

The men took them too seriously. Right now there was an ugly, sullen challenge in the overtones of the game in progress. Uncle Luther was right—the game was a conflict of will and character.

"Who is winning?" said a soft-edged voice from behind her.

Jacquelyn turned to stare directly into Natalie's face. Her cheeks flamed involuntarily. Was it from shame at feeling jealous of Natalie, whose beauty had attracted Scott?

"At this point, it is still anybody's game," Uncle Luther said, rising as his turn came around again.

Natalie's eyes stayed fixed on Jacquelyn. She gave Jacquelyn a challenging look from under long, curved eyelashes. "Will you be here for a long visit, Jacquelyn?" she asked slowly.

Jacquelyn raised her chin in an answering gesture of defiance. "Perhaps," she replied noncommittally. "I may even move back for a while. Uncle Luther wants me to help him restore the main wing of Cypress Halls."

Natalie smiled, but her fingers drummed nervously on her thigh. She obviously was covering up a lot of inner tension. What a shame, Jacquelyn thought distantly. She and Natalie had once been close friends. Even the undercurrent of rivalry between them during adolescence had not driven them apart. But now . . .

Suddenly, Natalie stood up and reached for Jacquelyn's hand. "Come on, Jackie. Let's go for a stroll through the garden." It was a bit of a jolt to hear Natalie call her by the familiar diminutive form of her name, as she had done when the two were children.

Jacquelyn hesitated. Natalie shot her a dark-eyed

expectant look. Slowly, Jacquelyn rose and followed.

"Remember how often we played hide-and-seek here when we were kids?" Natalie asked lightly. She reached up and touched a honeysuckle blossom.

"It was a real jungle in those days," Jacquelyn replied, remembering vividly those carefree days long since gone.

Natalie sighed. "Too bad we can't always stay children." She turned to Jacquelyn abruptly. "Life was so much simpler. We loved each other then, didn't we, Jacquelyn?"

"Of course," Jacquelyn replied, trying to recall the close, intense feelings she had once held for Natalie. "We were just like sisters, Natalie. I still love you," she confessed, searching her feelings and finding the old affection still lingered on, in spite of the circumstances.

Natalie broke off the honeysuckle blossom and rubbed it between her fingers. She was gazing at Jacquelyn steadily, her eyes filling with dark shadows. "But you've come back to take Scott away from me," she said softly.

"Oh, Natalie," Jacquelyn said impatiently. "How can you think such a thing? You know what was between Scott and me is over . . . forever."

The finality of her words brought a strange, hurting pang, but she knew it was true.

She wondered how much Natalie knew about the reasons for the chasm between her and Scott? Certainly Natalie knew about the fight Jacquelyn and Scott had had over her desire to work for a year before settling down to marriage. But did Natalie know any of the details of Scott's running Gerrard out of business?

On the one hand, Natalie and Gerrard had been so close, it would be hard to believe Gerrard had left without telling Natalie the details of what Scott had done to his business career. But on the other hand, how could Natalie have turned to Scott after Gerrard left? Surely the dark-haired girl must still be nursing a broken heart over the sad ending of her dreams of marrying Gerrard. She would have been as bitter toward Scott as Jacquelyn was if she knew the truth about him: that he had ruthlessly destroyed Gerrard's business career.

Jacquelyn remembered her conversation with her brother just before he left. He had not indicated that he'd told Natalie anything about the details of his business failure. Probably, his pride wouldn't let him.

But how could she tell Natalie the truth about Scott now? Her childhood friend would suspect her motives, thinking she was making up the story out of jealousy. No, that part would remain a secret in her heart. Natalie would just have to find out about Scott for herself.

"I'm not sure it *is* entirely over between you and Scott," Natalie persisted. "If a woman once loves a man—really loves him, I mean—is it ever over?"

"It certainly is between Scott and me," Jacquelyn insisted grimly.

Natalie's dark eyes measured Jacquelyn, not believing her. "I loved your brother, Gerrard, since we were children," she murmured, "and I lost him. At first I hated him for leaving me that way. After a while, I just didn't care any more. But I'm not sure what would happen if I ever came face to face with him again."

An unexpected rush of tears blurred Jacquelyn's

eyes. The rivalry between them was momentarily forgotten as her heart went out to her lifelong friend. "Natalie, I'm so sorry that things didn't work out between you and Gerrard—"

Natalie shrugged. "It doesn't matter. I told you I got over him some time ago."

"Do you ever hear from him?"

"No . . . do—do you?"

Jacquelyn wondered how truthful Natalie was being with herself. Did she still have a vulnerable spot buried in her heart where Gerrard was concerned, just as Jacquelyn could still feel her emotions storm when she was around Scott?

For a moment, the heartbreak they had both experienced drew her closer to the dark-haired girl. She experienced a moment of the love and understanding they had once shared.

But then Natalie closed the door between them with a challenging flash of her black eyes. "I just want you to know," she said, "that I've buried whatever I felt for Gerrard. Scott is the man in my life, now. I was in love with Gerrard as a child. I'm in love with Scott as a woman."

What did she mean by that? Jacquelyn wondered with an unexpected return of a jealous sting. She was implying an intimacy between her and Scott. How far had the intimacy gone? Jacquelyn shied away from pursuing that line of thought.

"I love Scott as a woman," Natalie repeated, an intense fire growing brighter in her luminous dark eyes. "And I mean to fight like a woman to keep him."

"I told you," Jacquelyn insisted, "I certainly have no designs on Scott McCrann. I want nothing more to do with him." She turned, wanting to leave.

But Natalie moved closer. Her hand closed painfully tight around Jacquelyn's wrist. Her eyes gazed straight into Jacquelyn's, the shadows in them deepening. "You always had the good things, Jackie. You lived in Cypress Halls and went away to college and had a glamorous career in New Orleans while Austin and I grew up in Aunt Perforce's little frame house in LaMere. But I'll never let you have Scott, Jackie. Remember that. . . ."

Natalie turned abruptly and disappeared down the graveled path, going back in the direction of the party, leaving Jacquelyn shaken by the intensity of her words. She glanced around at the thick hedges, the dark hiding places where they had played as children. That seemed a very long time ago, now.

It was near sundown when Uncle Luther got Natalie off in the house for a discussion and most of the guests had left. Jacquelyn sat in a lawn chair, staring off at the pink sunset smeared in light, puffy layers across the far horizon.

Suddenly, Scott appeared behind Jacquelyn. He held a drink in his hand. Even before she saw him, she felt his presence and stiffened. He stepped in front of her, his blue eyes brooding and dark. He looked down at her for a long minute. Her breath stopped. Her heart picked up tempo. Then he walked away from her, as if signaling her to follow him. He stopped by a far hedge, his eyes issuing a challenge to her.

Could she risk talking to him alone in the seclusion of the garden, conscious of the storm of emotions such an encounter would create? But hadn't she assured Natalie that she no longer had any interest in Scott? That was true, wasn't it? What they'd once had was damaged beyond repair. So what harm was there in talking to the man? If they were going to be working together on the restoration of the mansion, she'd have to force herself to be civil to him.

Besides, the gleam in Scott's eye was a dare, and Jacquelyn was not about to let him know how truly hurt she felt over what had happened between them. She would never again give Scott the powerful weapon of the knowledge of how deep her love for him had been. It was much too easy to use that kind of weapon against her.

She stood up, her knees shaking. She walked over to Scott, forcing herself to smile. "Had enough roque for today?" she asked.

"Yes," he said a bit harshly. "The way your Uncle Luther and I play it, it finally turns into a duel. I've had enough of that to last me a lifetime."

What did he mean by that, Jacquelyn wondered. She sensed he was talking about more than just the roque game.

"I don't like duels either," she said a bit sharply, wondering if he caught the full intent of her words.

"Even when you initiate them?" he asked pointedly.

So, she mused bitterly, he still held her responsible for their breakup. He obviously was not a man who forgot easily when his pride had been wounded. Would he seek even more revenge? she wondered with a sudden chill.

She chose the safe route of brushing his remark aside, pretending to miss his point. "Uncle Luther told me about your deal," Jacquelyn said, abruptly changing the subject. As she did so, she looked Scott full in the face. The light of the fading sun cast a tantalizing pattern of shadows on his face, making his deep blue eyes appear to smolder with intensity. It was the look he had used on her so many times in the past, the expression that had always melted her heart, flooding her with overwhelming love . . . until her eyes had been opened to his true nature and love had died.

But this time, that look on Scott's face was not of his own doing. It was the result of tricks played on his face by the rays of the setting sun. She reminded herself that they were no longer the same couple who had once been so much in love. Rather, they were two adversaries, and she must not read any of her own interpretations into Scott's behavior. She had to remember what kind of man he really was.

"And have you decided to restore Cypress Halls?" Scott asked.

"Yes," she said, answering his challenge with a steely resolve. "Why wouldn't I?" Her eyes blazed, daring him to tell her she couldn't take on the job.

For a long moment, Scott didn't answer, as if measuring his reply. Then he said, "I had wondered if you were willing to give up your freedom in New Orleans to come back here for an extended period."

His words puzzled her. "Are you saying you had something to do with Uncle Luther's wanting me to do the restoration?"

"Certainly not. As a matter of fact, I was against the idea from the start. But your uncle can be a stubborn man, and your accident provided him with the golden opportunity to persuade you to stay and take on the job."

Sudden anger flared in her. "You sound as if you don't think I'm qualified to take on this assignment."

"Only you know the answer to that," he said coolly.

"I certainly do, and let me assure you that I know perfectly well what I am doing!"

"If you did, I doubt that you would have come back."

Something in his tone unnerved her. Did his words carry some kind of threat? Or was her imagination becoming distorted by her tense emotions?

She clasped her hands, which had suddenly become icy, and spoke in measured tones to cover her inner turmoil. "I have as much right to be here as you. In fact, more right. I grew up here. My family has lived here for generations. You are the outsider who moved here."

His lips twisted in a sardonic smile as his eyes burned into her with a gaze that made her feel as if she were shriveling inside. "You seemed to welcome my moving here . . . until you got a taste of the outside world and decided your independence was more important."

"I have no desire to bring up the past," Jacquelyn said icily. "As far as I'm concerned, it's buried forever. I'd prefer to keep it that way."

"Do you think we can really bury the past?" he asked in a threatening tone. "Do you know how closely we're going to have to work together, you and I?" He reached out and took her by the arm.

For a moment, Jacquelyn was stunned. She couldn't understand why Scott was behaving like this. Then the realization hit her. Of course. He wanted to run her off. He didn't want her to restore the mansion. He felt the same deep bitterness toward her that she felt for him, and he hoped to intimidate her so badly that she'd change her mind and leave. It was going to be just as painful for him to work with her as it was going to be for her to work with him.

So much the better, she thought, chuckling to herself at the irony of the situation. Scott had made her miserable by his revenge on Gerrard. Now, she had an opportunity to make him miserable in return. But there was a big difference. She was not motivated by revenge. She was here only because of her warm love for Uncle Luther. She was willing to put up with almost anything to help Uncle Luther realize his lifelong dream, even if it meant being exposed to Scott McCrann.

"I'm staying!" she said obstinately.

Jacquelyn stood with her chin held high in a gesture of defiance.

Suddenly, Scott's arms encircled her. He pulled her to him. His strong embrace squeezed the breath out of her. He gave her a menacing look, and then his mouth came down on hers. It was a hard kiss, full of anger and resentment. It was a kiss that spoke of unrelieved frustration.

For a moment, Jacquelyn gloried in the pain she knew Scott had suffered because of her rejection of him. A man like that, who was ruthless and would stop at nothing to punish those who defied him, deserved the torment.

But then Scott's mouth turned softer, more insistent and demanding, and she recognized the kiss of passion. She tried to pull back her head. She struggled in his arms to free herself, but his hold on her was relentless.

Before she knew what was happening to her, she found herself wanting to return his kiss. A smoldering desire that had never been entirely squelched began to flame again. His lips demanded a response, and for an insane moment, she wanted to blindly forget her hatred of Scott, cancel out the past and respond with abandon.

Just then, a branch broke underfoot. The cracking noise caused Scott to release his hold on Jacquelyn. They both turned instinctively in the direction of the sound.

Natalie stood staring at them, her black eyes wide with shock. She opened her mouth as if to speak, but before the girl could say anything, Jacquelyn bolted past her and ran for the mansion, her throat tight with suffocated sobs.

She stumbled through the open doorway and saw the staircase through a blur of tears. She scurried upstairs and ran to her room, slamming the door behind her.

Her lips burned with the pain of Scott's kiss. And her heart ached with the memory of forgotten passion. How could she have let herself succumb to Scott's embrace, to his physical attraction? She knew what kind of man he was underneath that lanky, appealing frame. His heart was carved from stone. His ego was colossal. All he cared about was himself and his own desires. His kiss had not been intended to reawaken in her the flame of love that had once burned deeply within her. It had been an act of revenge, stirring her baser longings into a turmoil to make her want him physically, to torment and confuse her. And she had fallen into his trap, momentarily forgetting all the misery he had caused her, turning herself over to the longing she felt as he held her in his arms. What a fool she had been! How could she ever face Scott again?

Almost as bad was the prospect of trying to

explain to Natalie what had happened. It was less than two hours ago that Jacquelyn had assured the girl that she had no designs on Scott. How could she possibly explain why Natalie had found the two of them kissing?

Had Jacquelyn secretly wanted Scott to kiss her? No! She refused to believe that she could still feel anything but hate for such a ruthless man. Yet she had accepted the challenge of talking to him alone, and that would be very difficult to explain away to Natalie.

The old jealousy was bound to surface, and neither of them would be objective about the incident. Oh, what a mess this whole situation had become!

Jacquelyn jerked her suitcase out of the closet and frantically began tossing her clothes inside, leaving a trail of dropped garments tangled on the edge of the bed. When she found her suitcase would not close over the knot of fabric, she sobbed with frustration.

What had ever possessed her to return to Cypress Halls? Why had Uncle Luther not told her from the first about his deal with Scott? Why had she harbored, even for a moment, any tender feelings for Scott?

All she had were questions. No answers.

The situation was intolerable. In spite of what she had told Uncle Luther, there was no way she could endure being around Scott. She was leaving tomorrow for New Orleans, never to see Scott McCrann again!

Chapter Four

Jacquelyn stared morosely at the breakfast plate Hattie placed before her, but nothing was registering in her brain except her decision to leave Cypress Halls and the shadow of Scott McCrann.

Glancing at Uncle Luther, who was seated across the table from her, she became aware of a twinkle in his faded blue eyes.

She heard him say, "To think of a Cordoway having a hand in the actual restoration of Cypress Halls. It's more than I'd hoped for. Your accident turned out to be a blessing in disguise, Jacquelyn. Not that I wouldn't give anything to have spared you that awful ordeal."

Please, Uncle Luther, don't make it harder for me to break the news to you that I'm not going to stay after all, she thought dismally.

Uncle Luther put his fork down and gave Jacquelyn a sharp look over the top rim of his half-moon reading glasses.

"Is something troubling you, Jacquelyn?" he demanded in his deep baritone. "Out with it." It was not the command of a nosy third party, but rather the expectation that whatever was bothering her was a rightful concern of his. She was under his roof now, and as the lord of the manor, he took charge of all problems and settled matters promptly to his own satisfaction. It was a pleasure afforded him by his position in Cypress Halls and it was a post he guarded jealously. The world outside the confines of the mansion was out of his hands. Uncle Luther had often waxed eloquent about the evils of the modern age. He had grave doubts that the outside world was fit to live in. But here in his own environment he maintained the old standards of decency that he revered. He was King Arthur and Cypress Halls was his Camelot, where justice reigned supreme.

"I don't know how to tell you, exactly, Uncle Luther . . ." Jacquelyn began, swallowing a bitter lump in her throat.

"It's Scott McCrann, isn't it?" Uncle Luther interrupted, his pointed question hitting its mark dead center. "I thought it was all over between you two. But at the party last night, I sensed the tension. You still care for him, don't you?"

"Of course not!" Jacquelyn retorted a little too quickly. "I got him out of my system long ago," she fibbed. "But he—he wants to have a say-so in every selection, give final approval. I thought I'd have a free hand. I just don't know if I can work under these conditions."

How could she tell Uncle Luther how disconcerted she was at the storm of warring emotions Scott could still cause in her? How could she reveal that Scott was out to exact even more revenge on her, that he had kissed her last night to show he could still call forth in her the old physical longing she had once felt for him?

"Are you telling me you've changed your mind, that you're not going to stay after all?" Uncle Luther asked with a note of dismay.

Concern wrenched Jacquelyn's heart at the sudden pallor on the old man's cheeks, the expression of pain in his eyes.

"I didn't say that," she hedged, wondering why her courage was deserting her.

She had lain awake half the night rehearsing a speech to Uncle Luther explaining why she must disappoint him and return to New Orleans. But in the reality of morning light, her resolve was weakening. How could she break this dear old man's heart? He had done so much for her and her brother, Gerrard.

"Then what *are* you saying?" Uncle Luther asked softly, taking her hand in his large ones and patting it gently.

"I—I'm just saying working with Scott isn't going to be easy. I—I don't want you to be disappointed if the restoration doesn't turn out the way you expect. If Scott ties my hands, if he doesn't give me carte blanche, I can't guarantee the results."

"Don't you worry one bit," Uncle Luther thundered. "I have some control over the restoration. If you and Scott have any disagreements over what you want to do, leave it to me. I can handle him. Now, is there anything else bothering you?" he demanded with a fierce scowl.

"No," Jacquelyn choked feebly. "Nothing."

"Good," Uncle Luther said, his scowl relaxing into a smile. He replaced her hand gently on the table and returned his attention to his breakfast.

Jacquelyn picked numbly at her poached egg. She knew she could no more let Uncle Luther down than she could forgive Scott McCrann. It was an impossible situation, one that was tearing her heart in two.

Her preoccupation was interrupted by the arrival of Austin D'Raulde.

"Ah, Austin," Uncle Luther said, smiling and rising. He pulled out a chair, indicating with a sweep of his hand that Austin should occupy it. "Good you could join us this morning."

Austin settled his slender frame into the chair. His gaze rested on Jacquelyn, reflecting a mixture of anticipation and uncertainty. "How are you this morning, Jacquelyn?" he asked. "Did you enjoy the party last night?"

She sensed that behind the question was his wanting to know how she had reacted to seeing Scott and Natalie together. She flushed involuntarily, wondering if Natalie had told him of catching Jacquelyn in Scott's arms.

"It was very nice," she replied evasively. "I appreciate Uncle Luther's thoughtfulness. I know he did it to make me feel at home." She smiled at her uncle, her heart filled with a warm affection that made her cowardly impulse to run away seem terribly selfish.

Austin and Uncle Luther returned her smile, and then the three of them concentrated on eating breakfast and engaging in inconsequential chatter about Austin's accounting business.

Austin had been Uncle Luther's business manager

for some while. But that occupied only part of his time. He had branched out by keeping books for other businesses and now had an established and growing accounting firm.

"I have customers in New Orleans," Austin told Jacquelyn. "I'm opening a new office there and plan to spend a few days a month in the city, picking up accounts from even larger concerns. I have two customers already and prospects for several more." The expression on Austin's face told Jacquelyn he hoped she was impressed.

"That's wonderful, Austin," she said, genuinely happy for him.

"As a matter of fact," he went on, "I'm going to run into New Orleans today to make some arrangements. Want to ride along?"

"Well, I could bring back some of my things," Jacquelyn replied thoughtfully. "I packed only enough for a few days, really. I miss some of my personal belongings, and since I'm going to be here awhile . . ."

"Good," Uncle Luther chimed in. "Then by all means go along, my dear. I do want you to feel comfortable here. This old house hasn't been the same without you. It's really wonderful to have you back."

Jacquelyn smiled feebly, thinking that her greatest desire was to complete the restoration of the mansion as quickly as possible and leave. As it was, she didn't know how she was going to stand Scott's presence for the duration of her work.

In a way, she felt she had been trapped in an intolerable situation from which there was no escape. Her conscience was her warden, for it was her love and her devotion to Uncle Luther that kept her from refusing his job offer. How could she live with the guilt if she denied his most cherished request?

And yet, there was the specter of Scott McCrann tainting the entire project. Almost as powerful as her guilt was her hatred of that man.

It was only because her love for Uncle Luther was stronger than her hate for Scott McCrann that she could swallow her negative emotions and stay.

After breakfast, Jacquelyn went upstairs to change. She slipped into a bright red blouse that contrasted with a blue denim skirt edged with matching red piping sewed into the flared gores. The tight waistband hugged her small frame and gave her the appearance of a teenager dressed in an adult's attire. While she was fully developed and shapely, she had the lean, compact body of her youth. Only after she swept her long dark hair up into a neat knot on top of her head and applied a touch of mascara to her large blue eyes did she approach looking her age. She stepped into high-heeled sandals with just her bare feet, for the muggy heat of New Orleans made wearing hose quite uncomfortable this time of year.

The next afternoon, Scott arrived unexpectedly at the mansion with Natalie in tow. Jacquelyn gasped as she rounded the staircase and ran right into the two of them.

"I've been looking for you," Scott said.

Jacquelyn's eyes darted from Scott to Natalie and her pulse raced a bit as she dreaded confronting Natalie after the episode in the garden. How could she ever explain what she had been doing in Scott's arms?

Worse was the prospect of having to cope with Scott. Would he make reference to what had taken place between them? Or would he pretend it had never happened? Apparently, he had convinced Natalie to overlook the incident. The possessive gleam in her eye said she still considered Scott her property.

"What about?" Jacquelyn asked, finding her courage fragmented. She had been determined not to let Scott intimidate her, but the unexpected encounter had taken her by surprise.

"We'll talk about it at supper," Scott said decisively, thereby closing the matter for now. "I want Uncle Luther to take part in this discussion, and he's tied up with Austin in his study."

"Good," Natalie exclaimed. "That will give Jackie and me some time together before supper." She reached out to take Jacquelyn's hand.

Jacquelyn flinched. Her eyes darted toward Scott, but his expression was impenetrable. She turned her gaze toward Natalie, whose dark eyes were glowing with a strange intensity.

Jacquelyn did not relish a confrontation with Natalie after the embarrassing situation of being caught in Scott's arms. But there was no way to avoid it.

"Where do you want to talk?" Jacquelyn asked reluctantly.

For an answer, the dark-haired girl gave her hand a tug and they strolled through the French doors and down the path to the garden.

Jacquelyn flushed when she saw that Natalie was leading them to the exact spot where Scott had kissed her the night of the party. She stopped and turned to face her childhood friend.

A gentle breeze stirred a lock of Natalie's hair that touched her forehead, emphasizing her wild beauty.

The coolness under the moss-draped oaks flanked by the long rows of hedges gave Jacquelyn a sudden chill. Or was it the deep pools of emotion swirling in Natalie's eyes?

She was reminded that although she had been close to Natalie all her life, there were times when she hardly knew her friend at all. There was a side of Natalie as wild and dark and tangled as the swamp that bordered Cypress Halls. At the moment it was impossible to plumb the depths of her black eyes.

Jacquelyn drew a breath. "We do need to talk," she sighed. "I've been trying to think how to explain this to you, Natalie. I want you to understand the truth. The other night, when you saw Scott kiss me—"

Natalie reached up and touched her fingers to Jacquelyn's lips. "Hush," she said softly. She turned and plucked a magnolia blossom. She turned it slowly in her fingers, gazing into the distance. "You don't need to explain anything, Jackie," she murmured. "I know exactly what happened. I really wasn't surprised. I knew it would happen. I just didn't know when."

She directed her gaze toward Jacquelyn. Her eyes appeared clouded now. "I'm afraid you're letting yourself in for a lot of heartbreak, Jackie. I know the kiss meant nothing—to Scott. You see, I've come to know him quite well. He was deeply hurt when you turned down his offer of marriage twice, first to finish school, then to work at your career in New Orleans."

"I didn't turn Scott down," Jacquelyn cried impatiently. "He should have understood that. I just wanted more time—"

Natalie shrugged. "Scott is hot-tempered and full

of pride. Strong men like him usually have strong egos, too. I don't know who was at fault in the quarrels you had. Perhaps Scott was being unreasonable. Perhaps you were. It doesn't matter. What does matter now is that Scott is in a threatening mood where you are concerned. I think you should know that."

"What do you mean?" Jacquelyn asked, eyeing her suspiciously.

"Simply that I think Scott is a dangerous, angry man who can be ruthless. He wants revenge, and he wants to satisfy his male pride. What better way for a man to triumph over a woman than to seduce her . . . have a passing affair. 'Use' her, I believe, was the Victorian word for it. Then walk away, leaving her to nurse a broken heart."

Jacquelyn's cheeks flamed. "Well, you can save your breath with that kind of warning, Natalie," she snapped. "I would as soon have an affair with a rattlesnake!"

Natalie's lips moved in a cool smile. "I wouldn't be too sure of myself, Jackie. Obviously, he still holds a powerful physical attraction for you. Given the right setting, the right moment . . ." She raised an eyebrow. "Who knows?"

"I know," Jacquelyn stormed. "And I know that's all a lot of fantasy—"

But then, she wondered at the same time, why had Natalie's warning struck such an icy chill in her heart?

"Okay," Natalie said. She tossed the flower in a fountain pool. "You're a grown woman. It's your life. I only thought you should be warned not to believe anything Scott tells you. I know you think I'm making all this up because I'm jealous. Perhaps I am, a little. But I love you, too, Jackie. We grew up like sisters. Perhaps we aren't as close as we used to be. Still, I wouldn't want you hurt. You're Gerrard's sister, and—" She caught herself abruptly, then raised her chin and met Jacquelyn's eyes with a challenging look. "You see, I know that anything that would happen between you and Scott would have no real meaning. He and I have an understanding."

"Understanding?" Jacquelyn gazed at her with a mixture of confused emotions.

"Yes," Natalie said coolly. "Scott and I are going to be married."

Chapter Five

Jacquelyn stared across the wide rosewood table set with silver candlesticks. Her gaze rested on Natalie, who wore a demure white lace dress with a heart-shaped neckline. It hinted of a wedding dress, and Jacquelyn was certain Natalie had worn it for that express reason.

Jacquelyn was oblivious to the spicy aroma of the seafood gumbo with its pungent wafts of onion and fish. Hattie bustled around the table, ladling the okra-thick liquid into the large soup bowls.

Everyone in the room was silent for a moment. Jacquelyn felt as if she were an observer to the scene rather than a participant as she let her gaze flit around the table. She didn't notice the arborescent floral wallpaper creating a garden effect, even though this was her favorite room in this wing of the mansion. She was too busy wondering how dinner would turn out with the six people present. First there was Natalie, who flashed Scott a demure smile before her triumphant gaze settled on Jacquelyn.

Next came Scott, who was determined to have a hand in the restoration of the mansion, in spite of Jacquelyn's objections. At the head of the table sat Uncle Luther, his bushy white hair neatly combed into place. Would there be open warfare between Scott and Uncle Luther over Jacquelyn's determination to redecorate Cypress Halls her way?

Then came Austin in his tight-necked business suit, his eyes combing over Jacquelyn from time to time, making her feel uneasy. But strangest of all was the presence of Aunt Perforce, whom Uncle Luther had insisted on inviting to celebrate the beginning of Jacquelyn's assignment. Uncle Luther, while tolerant of her horoscoping, had always thought her almost as crazy as she thought him. It was as if the restoration of the old house had served as a catalyst to bring the whole family together once again. It erased all their differences and allowed them this one night together with everyone focused on their common goal, the refurbishing of Cypress Halls.

To the casual observer, it was a respectable family dinner with loved ones gathered around the table to share both a delicious meal and an evening of fellowship. But to Jacquelyn, it was an ordeal to be endured.

She was reviewing in her mind her conversation with Natalie in the garden, trying under her cool exterior to adjust to the emotional turmoil it had caused. Were wedding plans between Scott and Natalie really that definite, or was that another one of Natalie's imaginative fantasies? With a sinking feeling that confused her, Jacquelyn was inclined to believe it was true. She could usually tell when Natalie was playing make-believe.

And then she thought about Natalie's warning. It had made her angry, and at first she had dismissed it as the invention of Natalie's jealousy. But second thoughts were telling her that she might do well to give it some prayerful consideration. It certainly was in keeping with what she now knew about Scott's ruthless, vindictive character.

Jacquelyn had arrived at the dining room with a forced air of bravado, repeating to herself that if Scott and Natalie were going to be married, that would be just fine. She would be relieved that he would be taken out of circulation and would cease to be a threat to her. But her confident air melted at the sight of Scott and Natalie together. They had been standing in front of a lush dining room window hung with Waverly silk draperies. The lavender material imparted an aura of romance to the couple.

Jacquelyn took herself in hand, admonishing herself for her feelings and telling herself that she simply had a trace of possessiveness remaining from the days when Scott had been hers. No matter how she hated him now, Scott had, after all, once been the love of her life. That was enough to stir conflicting feelings over a marriage between Scott and Natalie.

But she could quickly replace those lingering feelings with a fresh wave of hate. For missing from the family gathering was the person who symbolized to her the black side of Scott's nature: her brother, Gerrard. If it had not been for Scott's savage desire for revenge, Gerrard would be with them now, happy and smiling, sharing this time together. He would be in one of the spoon-back chairs with their horsehair seats, eating from the Old Paris china that Uncle Luther and Hattie prized. They would be here together in the faded elegance of the old mansion, under the gilt, ormolu and tole chandelier suspended above the dining room table.

Such thoughts, with their poignant tug at Jacquelyn's emotions, rekindled her anger at Scott and chased away any lingering regrets she might have let herself feel about losing him.

The chatter around the dinner table was light. But there existed an undercurrent of tension that Jacquelyn was sure each of them felt. Austin's gaze alternated between Scott and Jacquelyn, obviously measuring Scott's impact on her. Uncle Luther ate with deliberateness. Jacquelyn sensed an uneasiness on his part about Scott and her having to work together. Natalie looked self-confident. Aunt Perforce sat back eyeing Jacquelyn, Natalie and Scott as if mentally casting their horoscopes and predicting dire consequences.

Jacquelyn carried the anxiety of the entire group in her stomach, which was a tight, hard knot. In spite of the cool summer breeze seeping in through the transom over the doorway, Jacquelyn felt clammy. Her pale yellow silk dress clung to her back and seemed unusually warm for this time of year.

Finally, when Hattie had cleared away the last of the dessert dishes and coffee had been served all around, Scott took charge of the conversation.

"I think it's time you made some definite plans, Jacquelyn," he said decisively.

"Plans? About what?"

"About the renovation. That is, if you've recovered sufficiently from your accident. We've delayed long enough. I'd like to get this matter under way."

There was a quality in his voice that infuriated her. So, he was going to start taking charge already, was he? Well, she'd just see about that!

"I've already begun," she replied tartly.

"Oh?" Scott said slowly, placing the coffee cup in its saucer with a hollow "chink."

Everyone else at the table seemed to fade into a hazy background as Scott's image across the table began to overwhelm the entire group. Jacquelyn's eyes were drawn to him against her will. But there was a magnetism about his commanding personality that forced her to give him her attention in spite of how much she loathed him. One thing she had to say for Scott McCrann: he could dominate any situation.

"And just what have you decided so far?" Scott demanded.

"I hardly think this is the place to discuss the restoration," Jacquelyn protested.

"This is the perfect place," Scott countered. "We're all family. Everyone is interested in your plans."

"Yes, Jacquelyn," Uncle Luther chimed in. "I didn't realize you had already started seriously thinking about what you're going to do. I'm eager to hear about it."

Jacquelyn gulped. How could she admit she had lied just to irritate Scott? She picked up her coffee cup and took a big slug of the hot liquid, which burned her throat as it washed down.

"Well," Jacquelyn replied, coughing, "first, I'm going to have to make several trips to New Orleans to locate the proper wallpaper for the south wing. I thought I'd start there." She put her cup down and swallowed a mouthful of water to chase away the last of the burning sensation.

"I'd like to go to New Orleans," Natalie exclaimed.

"All right," Scott replied accommodatingly. "We'll all go tomorrow."

"Wait a minute," Jacquelyn protested. "I didn't say I was ready to go to New Orleans tomorrow." The way Scott was taking over made her blood simmer.

"Then when will you be ready to go?" he asked, his blue eyes like rapiers slicing away at her determination not to let him control her.

"In a few days."

"Fine, we'll go the first of next week," Scott replied, as if the matter were settled.

"Good," Austin cut in. "I need to check on my branch office there, so I'll join you. We can make it a foursome."

Jacquelyn shot Uncle Luther a helpless look, begging him to come to her rescue. But he smiled indulgently, as if the plans shaping up against Jacquelyn's will had been all her idea. Then Jacquelyn looked at Aunt Perforce, whose black eyes flitted between Jacquelyn and Scott. The smug expression on her face said she knew trouble had been inevitable.

"I'll go by myself," Jacquelyn said flatly. "I like to be alone when I work."

"You can be alone all you want when you work," Scott replied. His tone indicated he was setting a trap. Jacquelyn had heard that vocal quality of his before.

"But . . . ?" Jacquelyn asked, calling his hand.

"But I will be there when you select the wallpaper. Remember, I have final approval of everything."

Jacquelyn's first impulse was to dump the entire project back in Scott's lap, to quit on the spot. She could not work with Scott looking over her shoulder. She was the interior decorator. She knew what she was doing. What right did he have to take charge like that?

But she stopped short of giving in to her anger when Uncle Luther interrupted. "Scott, Jacquelyn is quite skilled at her work. I'm sure whatever she selects will be perfect. Remember, she grew up in this old house; she has a special feeling for it. I will not have her inhibited. She must feel free to restore it as she sees fit."

The tension seemed to melt in Scott, and he leaned back in his chair and sat quietly for a moment.

Jacquelyn realized this was to be just the first in a long series of conflicts. Each round would be a source of irritation, with her at Scott's throat and Uncle Luther forced into the role of arbitrator. Was it really to the old man's benefit to have her redecorate the mansion under these trying circumstances?

"Of course," Scott agreed. "That was understood from the beginning. But it was also understood that I held final approval of her selections."

A stony silence settled on the group. Jacquelyn realized a silent duel was taking place between Scott and Uncle Luther. Both were strong-willed, determined men. Neither wanted to come out the loser. Each possessed an ego of enormous strength. But where Scott was hard and ruthless, Uncle Luther was kind and warmhearted.

Suddenly, Jacquelyn realized she was the key to the solution of this round of the battle. If she sat silent, Uncle Luther might well lose to Scott by default. If she let Uncle Luther defend her position so strongly that he and Scott came to a parting of the ways, her uncle would never see his dream come true. Scott was just hardhearted enough to use her as leverage to force Uncle Luther's hand. Scott was not beyond insisting that either Jacquelyn do the remodeling or he would renege on the deal.

Why was Scott behaving in such a savage manner? She had to believe that vengeance was his motive. Her rejection of his offer of marriage must have wounded his pride so deeply he could not forget or forgive. Where he had once loved her ardently, now anger and bitterness burned with the same degree of passion. Weren't hate and love closely related? Apparently, running her brother out of business hadn't been enough; he had to strike at her directly.

He had engineered this situation so that no matter what she did she was bound to be hurt. If she stayed and let Scott walk all over her, she was going to suffer emotionally. But if she refused to restore the mansion, she would be overwhelmed with guilt for disappointing Uncle Luther.

"I know you have final approval," Jacquelyn conceded at last, shooting Scott a murderous stare. "But I don't need your help in making my selections. After I have decided on suitable wallpaper, then you can give your approval." She demanded at least that much of a concession.

"Of course," Scott said. "That's what I had in mind."

"Of course," Uncle Luther agreed, as if the solution had been clear from the first. The old man looked relieved.

"But," Scott added, obviously determined to have the final word, "I'm going to New Orleans next week, and you might as well come along and begin looking. I insist on it."

"If you say so," Jacquelyn agreed stiffly.

She was spared any further contact with Scott or Natalie until the day of the trip to New Orleans.

That morning, she dressed with a feeling of apprehension. No matter what she wore, Natalie would be sure to think she was trying to capture Scott's attention.

She determined to look as businesslike as possible. She knotted her straight dark hair in a bun on top of her head, touched her lashes with mascara and smoothed her linen dress down over her shapely hips. The ecru-colored garment met just above her breasts in a wide V that gave just a hint of sophistication. She strapped a thin brown belt around her waist and stepped into tan heels which matched her purse.

Austin met her at the foot of the stairs and escorted her out to Scott's gold-colored Lincoln. Jacquelyn braced herself for the tension that would mount when the four of them began their drive into New Orleans. Scott was behind the wheel. Natalie sat close beside him. Jacquelyn and Austin settled into the plush gold crushed velvet seats in the back. Soft music played through rear deck speakers. A draft of cool air enveloped them, softly protecting them from the warm humidity outside.

As she suspected, the conversation during the ride was strained. She felt a sense of relief when Scott dropped her and Austin off at his branch office. Natalie planned to do some shopping while Scott went off to take care of several business matters. But before driving off, he insisted on settling on a time to meet Jacquelyn later on Royal Street, where she would be embarking on her plans to renovate the mansion.

The brittle wire of tension broke as soon as she saw his gold Lincoln merge with the downtown traffic and disappear.

She spent a little time with Austin at his office. Then she took a taxi to the French Quarter to begin browsing for pieces she planned to use in refurbishing the Cordoway mansion.

Most of the antique shops were located on Royal Street. She wandered in and out of several smaller stores, keeping her eyes open for accent pieces such as vases, mirrors, rugs and chandeliers. These were the objects that would be the hardest to find. The larger furniture, such as beds, sideboards, an armoire and tables, she could probably find at Morton's, where auctions were held on a regular basis.

In one small shop jammed with antiques, rare books, old magazines and Persian rugs, Jacquelyn found a perfect mahogany tripod table with a piecrust top. The table, with a pedestal supported by three outturned legs, was in mint condition. The price was a steal, and Jacquelyn had struck a deal before she had even given a second thought to Scott. It was only after she had left the shop and was proceeding down Royal Street that she remembered the black cloud hanging over this entire project. Scott McCrann and his wretched final approval!

She knew him. If she admitted to having already taken the table, he would turn thumbs down just to humiliate her. So she would have to pretend she had not already told the shopkeeper to tag it as sold. When they went to pick it up, she'd have to stand back and let Scott have his little inspection, as if she were waiting for his go-ahead. What a rotten game she was going to have to play. And she could see it was going to be like this through the entire project.

Could she really work under these circumstances?

The enthusiasm with which Jacquelyn had begun her trip was dampened by the specter of Scott constantly looking over her shoulder.

When she located a rare Georgian knife box from the 1700s, again Jacquelyn's ire grew as she realized how easily she could lose this unique piece. Once again she struck a bargain with the shopkeeper, determined that she would find a way to pay for this ancient treasure, even if Scott disapproved. How she hated the deception.

It was late in the afternoon when Jacquelyn and Scott met as agreed. She stood at the corner of Jackson Square, near the high wrought-iron fence that surrounded the park. Artists displaying their works lined the wide sidewalk that bordered the park. Tourists strolled by the paintings, making comments. Occasionally, someone paid for a canvas and carried it away, wrapped in brown paper and tied with a string.

One portrait painter drew a young girl in pastels as she sat on a wooden chair in the weary light of the dying sun. Deftly, the artist's hands zipped across the canvas, streaking shades of muted crimson and lavender in the background. The girl sat silently in the chair as if posing for a time exposure photograph.

Suddenly, Jacquelyn felt a hand on her elbow. She had the impression that the rainbow of colors on the painting in front of her had jumped off the canvas and shot into her. She jerked around, knowing it was Scott before looking at him.

A breathless feeling gripped her. She had known

he was coming, but she hadn't expected him to intrude on her concentration so brazenly. Couldn't he have said her name before he touched her? It was just like him, she thought sourly. He was always determined to take charge in his own way with no thought for how he affected others.

"Have any luck?" he asked, leading her toward a little café across the street. "You can tell me what you found over a cup of coffee."

"You know some antiques are in great demand, don't you?" she retorted sharply. "They are quickly snatched up. I don't have time to dawdle over coffee. I want to go back and let you give your royal approval *now.*"

Her angry words had spilled out of their own volition.

"My! Caustic, aren't we?" Scott murmured.

Jacquelyn bit her tongue. Losing her temper might give Scott the upper hand. If she allowed her hostility to show, Scott might retaliate by becoming stubborn and refusing to accept the pieces she had picked out today.

"Just trying to be businesslike," she said, making an effort to hide her resentment under softer tones.

"All right," he said. "We'll go look at your selections."

Jacquelyn was surprised at his agreeability. She had expected a tougher fight. Maybe he was waiting until they reached the shops to refuse to pay for what she had chosen.

As they headed back to Royal Street, Jacquelyn couldn't resist a sideways glance at Scott. She had to admit a grudging admiration for his physique—the broad, straight shoulders, the erect carriage of his lanky frame. She observed his long, agile fingers and recalled how they had skillfully and tenderly massaged suntan lotion on her back when they had still been in love.

The waning sun drifting behind the buildings cast a soft purple glow over Scott's unruly brown hair, lending him an aura of mystery and intrigue. For an instant, Jacquelyn saw him as a stranger, as a man strolling beside her whom she had never known.

Was he really the heartless villain she had painted him? Could a man with muted shadows playing across his face in such a tantalizing fashion harbor deep in his heart such a hatred for her that he would purposely run her brother out of business?

Scott ambled along quietly, his arms swinging back and forth rhythmically. There was an almost musical quality to the way he moved, like a chorus from one of the melodious Dixieland tunes that floated from the open doors of the clubs on Bourbon Street. He marched in cadence, smoothly, lithely, like a well-trained jungle animal exercising itself for the pure pleasure of the stretching of muscle tissue. Never before had Jacquelyn noticed this earthy quality in Scott, and it sent a shiver tickling down her spine. Goose bumps popped out all over her, and she shuddered involuntarily.

At the two shops, Scott very agreeably paid for Jacquelyn's selections, which they would pick up later.

Maybe working with him wasn't going to be so awful after all, Jacquelyn mused as they headed for a small coffee shop. She had certainly expected more opposition from him, if for no other reason than just to antagonize her. But he seemed genuinely pleased with her choices.

They stepped past a couple standing on the sidewalk leaning against a wooden post and listening to the Dixieland band warm up. Many of the clubs, cafés and bars provided almost continuous entertainment for their customers, and the open doors allowed would-be patrons to sample the style of music before entering.

Scott led Jacquelyn into a tiny coffeehouse next door to a café with a lively band. He escorted her to a booth and directed her to sit down.

A waitress placed two glasses of water in front of them and gave them a quizzical glance. "Menus?" she asked.

"No, just coffee," Scott replied. "Is that all right?" he asked almost as an afterthought, glancing at Jacquelyn.

In any other frame of mind, Jacquelyn would have ordered something else just to assert herself. But Scott seemed so easy to be around now, she hadn't the motivation for any type of rebellion.

"Coffee's fine," she murmured.

The waitress moved away from the table. Jacquelyn felt a sense of their aloneness engulf them and she frowned at the vulnerable sensation rippling through her.

Scott settled down on the padded bench seat of the booth, sending little shock waves of warmth her way. He twisted slightly to get a better look at her, and as he did so, his hand brushed hers. She jerked it back instinctively and then regretted her action.

Scott's eyes played over her face. The intensity of the blue of his irises was magnified by a little lamp behind them.

Little snatches of anxiety zipped through Jacquelyn. It was dangerous to let herself feel this way around Scott. Was he purposely trying to reawaken in her the old feelings she had once cherished and mooned over? Surely it was no accident that he had touched her hand with his. He was too calculating a man for that.

The coffee arrived. Silent for a time, they sipped the potent Louisiana brew with its heavy chicory flavor. Jacquelyn stole a moment of sheer pleasure in reverie as she allowed her once vital love for Scott to replay briefly in her mind. Was Scott remembering, too?

"Well," Scott said at last. "The renovation is starting out better than I expected."

His words dispelled her moment of sentimental reflection, replacing the mood with a more realistic suspicion of everything Scott said. "What do you mean?"

"I mean you found two suitable items for the mansion today."

"Of course. That's what I'm trained to do. I'd say the things I found are more than suitable—they're perfect."

"Yes, I agree. They're perfect."

Why was he being so agreeable? she wondered. It was almost as if he had reverted for the moment to the man she had remembered . . . before she had found out about the ruthless side of his nature.

"I'm glad matters are starting out well," Scott said, "because I have arranged for several contractors who can begin work almost immediately. I thought I'd have them begin with the old ballroom."

"The old ballroom?" Jacquelyn echoed, suddenly feeling an agitation that caused her fingers to restlessly fold and unfold the corner of her napkin.

"Yes, it needs a great deal of repair before you can even begin your part of the job."

"I thought every element of the restoration was part of my job," Jacquelyn protested.

"Nothing was said about letting you oversee the heavy repairs," Scott said.

"But I just assumed . . ." Jacquelyn began, her anger beginning to rise.

"That's not a job for a woman," Scott cut in.

"Mr. McCrann," Jacquelyn said evenly, trying to control the hostility bubbling up in her, "I have worked with several contractors on every phase of remodeling you can imagine. I know rebuilding from the inside out. While I'm not very good at wielding a hammer myself, I can instruct a workman where to pound every nail. I know who's competent in this business and who's not. I have people I like to work with, and I will select my own contractors." Jacquelyn angrily crushed her napkin and threw it down beside her empty coffee cup as she rose.

Scott smiled condescendingly. He took a swig of coffee before replying, as if considering his answer.

When he spoke, his voice was soft but authoritative. "I am in charge, Jacquelyn. Don't forget. In essence, you are working for me."

Scott slid out of the booth and offered Jacquelyn his hand, which she ignored. She marched ahead of him out of the café, not pausing by the cashier's desk as Scott paid the bill.

Out on the sidewalk in the warmth of the late afternoon, Jacquelyn's ire grew. It was bad enough that Scott had put her in an untenable position. But his superior attitude was like pouring salt in a raw wound. He didn't have to be so unbearably arrogant about the entire matter.

When he joined her, Jacquelyn turned her face away from Scott and refused to look in his direction.

For a few moments, as they walked side by side, Scott remained silent. Then he spoke. "You're just making this more difficult for yourself."

"What does that matter to you?" she said crossly.

"I just thought you might want to enjoy the trip a little more," he said casually.

"This trip would have been perfect if I had come alone," Jacquelyn replied bitingly.

"Oh, this is not the trip I'm talking about," Scott said mysteriously.

"Then just what trip do you mean?" Jacquelyn hated herself for jumping at Scott's bait. But curiosity overshadowed pride.

"The one you and I are going to take," he said, obviously enjoying his little game.

"I don't know what you're talking about."

"Of course you don't," Scott replied with a low chuckle. "But you're just dying to know, aren't you?"

"Not in the least!"

"That's funny," Scott said slowly. "I seem to recall an innate curiosity in your nature. That's not a trait that can be turned off like a sprinkler."

Suddenly, Jacquelyn turned on Scott and stared straight into his face. The light glinted on a wisp of his unruly brown hair. A couple brushed past them on the sidewalk, casting them a cursory glance.

"Will you get to the point?" she demanded.

Scott rubbed his hands together in satisfaction. The long, tapered fingers slid past each other smoothly.

"It's very simple," Scott said, his lips curling into a knowing smile. "I have to make an extended business trip. You will come along and look for furnishings for the mansion."

"Why should I?" Jacquelyn asked defiantly. "I can find most everything I need here in New Orleans."

"Because I'm going to a very special place," Scott replied, his smile widening.

"Where?" Jacquelyn challenged him. There was no spot in the entire United States where she would go with *him*. It had been enough of an ordeal to drive into New Orleans in his company. An overnight trip was out of the question.

"Paris," Scott said.

"Paris?" Jacquelyn gasped. Paris! An interior decorator's dream for refurbishing a place like Cypress Halls. The treasures she could find there made her heart race with excitement. She might find authentic pieces from the Louis XVI period, or perhaps even the Regency era. Chairs, beds and other kinds of furniture that could be found only in museums in the United States might still be available for purchase in Europe.

"Interested?" Scott teased.

"I might be." Jacquelyn shrugged, making a supreme effort to disguise her excitement.

"I thought so," Scott murmured, turning to stroll down the sidewalk and leaving Jacquelyn in the disadvantaged position of having to hurry to catch up with him.

It was a psychological ploy she detested. He was determined to make her run after him. How he must love the superior air it gave him to have Jacquelyn at his heels! It was a trick to manipulate her.

Suddenly, Jacquelyn stopped. Her high heels no longer clicked brittlely along the pavement behind Scott. He took a few more steps, hesitated and then turned. "Coming?" he asked, his blue eyes raking her mockingly.

"No," she answered emphatically.

"You mean you're turning down a trip to Paris?"

"That's not what I meant and you know it!" She fumed, tapping her right toe angrily on the sidewalk. She was determined not to let him get the best of her. "I mean I'm not going to trail behind you like a puppy dog."

"Then come on," Scott ordered and turned his back on her, striding briskly past the shops and cafés toward his car.

"Ooh!" Jacquelyn exclaimed in disgust. How she would love to yank off a high heel and hurl it at the back of Scott McCrann's arrogant head. She imagined it hitting its mark and sending pain shooting through him. That would be nothing compared to the anguish he had caused her, and it would serve him right. But she suppressed her impulse.

Instead, she hurried after Scott, determined to catch up with him. Her eyes were narrow with hostility. He had won this round, and they both knew it. He must be feeling rightly smug, she thought bitterly.

But it wasn't this round that really had her worried. It was the next one, the one that really mattered, when they were in Paris together.

Paris was the city of lovers. It symbolized romance the world over. Was Scott truly interested in the antique treasures she might find in France? Or was he planning to carry out the scheme Natalie had warned her about?

In Paris, Jacquelyn would be dependent on Scott. She spoke no French, really. She knew only a few phrases she had picked up along with her Louisiana heritage. She was not widely traveled or sophisticated. Would she succumb to the magic of Paris and to the phony charms of Scott McCrann? She knew from personal experience how disarming Scott could be when he chose to sweep a girl off her feet.

Paris was the perfect spot for Scott to complete his plan to use Jacquelyn, to satisfy his physical craving for her left over from their shattered romance and then to toss her aside.

Would she be able to resist him in that kind of romantically charged atmosphere?

Jacquelyn hated herself for her weakness where Scott was concerned. But she could never let him know about it. So she would go to Paris and pray for the strength to rebuff him. She must keep in the forefront of her mind what kind of man he really was.

Yes, she would go. But she was afraid.

Chapter Six

"Don't go, Jacquelyn," Aunt Perforce had warned in ominous tones. "There will be nothing but trouble for you if you make that trip to Paris."

They had been sitting at the table in her aunt's kitchen, where Aunt Perforce had spread out her horoscope charts.

"It's going to be all right," Jacquelyn had reassured her aunt. "Natalie and Austin are going on the trip, too, so Scott and I will not be thrown together alone. I'm not worried." It was only a small fib. When Natalie had heard about the trip she had insisted on going. Next, she engineered a vacation for Austin. Jacquelyn felt sure Natalie wanted her brother along for less than altruistic reasons. With Austin to keep Jacquelyn company, Natalie would have Scott all to herself.

Now, on the plane headed for Paris, Jacquelyn recalled her aunt's prediction and wondered if the woman had been right. Shadowy doubts plagued her heart.

Everything had gone too smoothly. Something was bound to go wrong. She felt it. And the sensation left her uneasy.

The carpentry work on the mansion had begun, with contractors swarming all over the place. The sounds of power saws, the aroma of saw dust and little trails of paint splattered over drop sheets characterized the activity at Cypress Halls for the weeks following Scott's announcement of the trip to Paris.

In New Orleans, Jacquelyn had found a beautiful birch and fruitwood secretary, an oak and mahogany bureau with a delicately shaded billet-chain banding and bird and stellate inlays, and a gilded and decorated black lacquer center table with ball-and-claw legs. Scott had approved all her selections and the pieces had been moved into one room of the mansion, where all the newly purchased items were being stored until the appropriate room was ready for them.

Jacquelyn had become so caught up in the restoration she forgot about her animosity for Scott. When he announced the date of their departure for France, Jacquelyn had packed eagerly. Only after the four of them had boarded the plane did Jacquelyn realize how close they would have to stay to each other for the duration of the trip. They would be strangers in a foreign land, seeking each other out for companionship and security. She was determined to lean on Austin for help, not Scott.

Scott had booked them into a first-class hotel. The room Jacquelyn and Natalie shared had two double beds, a TV set hung on the wall and a spectacular view of the city.

They spent the first couple of days simply being tourists. They went up the Eiffel Tower, toured Notre Dame and took the obligatory boat trip down the River Seine. They visited Montmartre, the one-time farming hamlet that had been swallowed up by the city over one hundred years ago. They walked its cobbled streets and ate in one of its quaint restaurants.

At breakfast on the third day they were seated in the hotel restaurant, surrounded by hungry tourists. Jacquelyn heard conversations in French, German, Chinese, and English with a British accent.

A uniformed waiter hovered near their table, his head cocked in anticipation of their order. His broken English brought a smile to Jacquelyn's lips.

Scott gave the order in almost perfect French. He had spent quite a bit of time traveling abroad on business trips the last few years and had a natural affinity for languages.

Jacquelyn had placed a map of Paris on the table. "I think it's time I made an excursion here," she said, tapping the map with her finger. "I've studied the tourist guides, and they list rue Bonaparte and rue la Boétie as the two main streets for antique shops."

"I want to stroll down the Champs-Elysées," Natalie interjected. "It's supposed to be the most famous thoroughfare in Paris. It runs right into the Arc de Triomphe." She shot Scott a pleading look.

"All right," he said. "Natalie, you and Austin take in some more tourist attractions. I have some business to tend to. I'll drop Jacquelyn off in the antique district. That way you can both see what appeals to you most. There's no reason for the four of us to stick together all the time.''

Right after breakfast, the four of them parted company.

It was only when Jacquelyn finally got away from the traditional views of Paris seen by visitors that she began to feel a part of this marvelous city.

Paris had a heartbeat all its own. It was a throbbing, vibrant city full of many types of people. Jacquelyn was eager to get to know it from a more intimate perspective.

Scott stood on the sidewalk and hailed a taxi. A small, boxy cab pulled up to the curb and Scott opened the door. Jacquelyn hopped in, settled down on the vinyl seat and then did a double take. A dark brown fuzzy head popped up on the passenger side of the front seat. It was a large dog who peered at her suspiciously over the seat. His brown eyes shifted to Scott as he settled in beside her.

Scott slammed the door, gave directions to the driver and leaned back. The cab pulled away from the sidewalk and ground into the heavy stream of cars whizzing past in the eight lanes of traffic of the wide boulevard.

Jacquelyn poked Scott in the ribs with her elbow and silently pointed to the dog.

Scott tentatively reached his hand toward the canine. It growled and bared its teeth. Scott withdrew his hand and spoke in French to the driver.

"The cabbie says the dog's name is Pierre," Scott explained. "He rides in the cab as protection. Also as company. The driver warned me that Pierre has a very short temper. He's old, like Paris, and unchanging.''

"Is he dangerous?"

"I don't think so," Scott replied. "Pierre is like most Parisians—he likes to appear gruff. Keep that in mind today and don't take it personally when you deal with shopkeepers. You'll be on your own in the antique district. Expect some of the store owners to be a bit abrasive. Some take pride in being the most irritable proprietors on the block. It's a little hard to grow accustomed to at first, but once you do, you'll find it a rather endearing trait. Sort of like little children trying to play a stern parent and not doing a very good job of it."

Scott chuckled. Jacquelyn realized how truly cosmopolitan he was.

Jacquelyn looked out the cab window and admired the beautiful chestnut trees lining the street and the colorful canopies over the many sidewalk cafés along the way.

She recalled Scott's assessment of Paris when they had first arrived. "In France," he had said, "everything is permitted, even what is forbidden. The French love to indulge themselves. They refuse to be bound by inflexible rules. They find discipline deadening.

"They love to enjoy life, to eat, drink, make love and wring the most out of each moment. They are incurable talkers. Most of all, they are charming and unforgettable. Once you've been to Paris, you can never get this city out of your heart."

Scott's voice had taken on a sentimental quality. Jacquelyn had not heard him speak in such tones since he had whispered endearments to her when they were dating. Little rivulets of nostalgia began cascading in her, washing away some of the resentment she felt for him.

To guard against further softening of her feelings, she directed her attention out the window. The traffic was thick with bicycles, scooters and mopeds weaving in and out between the cars. At an intersection controlled by a jaunty-looking policeman, the cab stopped. Jacquelyn was fascinated by the peaked cap angled over one eye and the snappy white gloves and white baton of the officer. His hands waved in rhythm to an imagined symphony as he twirled, directing the other lanes of traffic to move on.

Just then a motorcycle edged its way to the front of the line of cars and stopped. Behind the driver sat a helmeted girl, her long dark hair streaming out from under the head protection. She suddenly removed her helmet, took off the driver's with her other hand and leaned around him, planting a hard kiss on his lips. Then she replaced their helmets just before the policeman twirled to wave them through the intersection, and the couple sped off, swallowed up in the rush of automobiles.

Jacquelyn smiled, self-consciously wondering if Scott had witnessed the scene. She turned her gaze to the sidewalk. There, couples strolled hand in hand. In doorways and under the chestnut trees, lovers hugged and kissed openly. It was a scene Jacquelyn had come to expect after only two days in Paris. Yet today, alone with Scott in the taxi, she felt more keenly aware of the casually displayed intimacy than she had when Austin and Natalie had been with them.

At last the cab came to a stop. Scott opened the door for her. She stepped out onto the sidewalk, breathing the Parisian air with its acrid hint of Gauloises, the popular French cigarette.

Jacquelyn saw a robust woman standing at the

entrance to an apartment house. She leaned heavily against the railing, her sharp-eyed inquisitiveness daring an intruder to pass. One arm was akimbo, fist ground pugnaciously into her waist. Her burgundy sweater, buttoned down the front, gaped open between the closures. She must be a concierge, thought Jacquelyn. A Parisian institution, these human security systems had been around since the Napoleonic era.

At last, she thought, she was going to get to see the real Paris.

She wanted to scour the antique district, to wander alone by herself. She enjoyed the challenge of seeing if she could cope in a strange country on her own. She had her maps, her little books of translated phrases that she could point to if necessary and plenty of francs.

"Sure you'll be okay?" Scott asked, stepping from the cab.

His look of genuine concern made her heart skip a beat. Momentarily, the feeling worried her. Was she falling under the spell of the city of love?

It was only natural that here in Paris, where romance was supreme, any nostalgic memories of her relationship with Scott would feel more poignant.

"I better go," she said, breaking the spell that threatened to engulf her. "I have a lot of looking to do."

"Good luck," Scott said, his eyes lingering on hers a moment too long.

Jacquelyn looked away. She had acknowledged that his gaze had disturbed her and she hated herself for letting Scott know she could still feel anything but contempt for him.

"I'll meet you for lunch," he offered.

"Where?" Jacquelyn asked.

She really didn't want to eat alone. It would be nice to have company, even if it meant subjecting herself to Scott.

"There."

Scott pointed to a green-and-white striped canopy across the street. The sidewalk café was half full of early morning patrons sipping coffee and chatting amiably. "Think you can find it?"

"Of course," Jacquelyn answered, smiling. She patted her tourist guides. "With all this, how can I miss it?"

The smiles they exchanged were warm. To a passerby, they would have appeared like any ordinary couple parting for the morning. But to Jacquelyn, they were two adversaries who had temporarily sheathed their weapons. Why she should be willing to call a truce this morning, she didn't know.

Scott climbed back in the cab, waved good-bye, and the taxi whisked him away from the curb.

For a moment, Jacquelyn felt a small wave of panic. She was alone in a foreign country where she could not speak the language. For all her bravado, it occurred to her that she could become lost. Of course, she could always phone the hotel, where there were English-speaking clerks.

The uneasiness subsided and she was soon lost in the grips of the intrigue of high adventure.

She strolled down the sidewalk, jostled from time to time by a passing shopper. The roar of automobiles, the honking of their horns, the strains of music from a violinist at a sidewalk café and the contrast of modern buildings juxtaposed to ancient gothic architecture transported Jacquelyn to a new, heady level of consciousness.

She walked slowly, almost hypnotized. The sun shone brightly, but the air was crisp and cool. She felt comfortable in her red and black suit of houndstooth-checked bouclé. The wraparound skirt was topped with a loose-fitting jacket, which she could remove if she felt too warm. But right now she was feeling just right, elated at the sense of freedom to explore Paris alone and go where she chose.

The street was lined with shops, most of which sported some sort of animal effigy as a symbol. There was a large bronze snail perched atop a black wrought-iron base that hung over a restaurant specializing in *escargots*. A butcher shop sported a large pig's head mounted over the door. Over one entrance, a monkey hung by his tail. Jacquelyn was surprised to look in the window and discover an antique shop.

When she opened the door, a little bell rang. It was dim inside. The shop was small and cluttered. Clocks, mirrors, dishes, knickknacks, silverware, vases and odd pieces of furniture were stacked around the room.

From the back of the store emerged a small, squinty-eyed man with a shock of sparce but wiry gray hair. He sported a thin, jaunty white moustache.

The man shuffled up to Jacquelyn, cast her a haughty stare and said something in French.

"Do you speak English?" Jacquelyn asked tentatively.

"English," the little man muttered with a thick accent. "Everybody wants English. You American?"

Jacquelyn nodded.

The little man dismissed her with a wave of his hand, as if she were beneath contempt.

"I'm looking for antiques," Jacquelyn said, hoping the prospect of a sale might capture the old man's interest.

"Then look," he said as if bored.

"I'm not sure I want to, if that's your attitude," Jacquelyn retorted, her ire rising.

"Suit yourself," the man said, picking up a small rag and flicking it across a set of cups and saucers on a low shelf.

He stirred up a dusty smell. Jacquelyn almost sneezed.

Scott had certainly been right, Jacquelyn mused. If this shopkeeper was typical, she was in for an interesting day. He was an old grouch. If he was vying for most abrasive dealer on the block, he'd definitely get her vote.

"You might get a few more customers if you were a little friendlier," Jacquelyn pointed out, noticing the lack of shoppers.

"Young lady," the little man said sharply, his eyes hard and piercing, "I run my business my way." Jacquelyn had to listen closely to understand his fractured English. "I sell at good prices, and all my antiques are genuine. I never try to pass off fakes. You may not like me, but you cannot dislike my wares. Look and you will see they are the finest in Paris. If you think you find better somewhere else, you go buy there. You will be the fool."

The little man's difficulty with English did not interfere with his ability to get his point across, Jacquelyn thought. Her first impulse had been to stalk out of the shop, insulted. But the more she talked to the little man, the more she realized his superior air covered up a certain kind of self-mockery. He obviously did not take himself all that seriously, and he must have expected her to make light of his retorts.

Once she understood that, Jacquelyn relaxed and began to enjoy the verbal jousting.

She picked up a clock that looked like a Louis XV doré cartel. It was ornately carved with a scantily clad figure on top.

"I'm sure you're asking too much for this," she said, joining in on the fun of haggling in the Parisian fashion. It was surprising how easy it was to fall in with the verbal stabs.

The little man smirked. "You would not appreciate that piece," he said, faltering over the word "appreciate." "It takes someone who knows about fine things."

Jacquelyn considered for a moment before she answered. Instinctively she understood how she should reply. "Maybe if you explained its value to me . . ." Jacquelyn ventured.

The little man looked directly at her. He placed his dusting rag on the counter. He reached for the clock and took it from her hands. Tenderly, he rubbed its surface. His eyes glinted as if from some long-ago memory.

"You really want to know?" he asked.

"Yes, I do," Jacquelyn answered.

"Then sit down," he ordered, pointing to a small straight-backed chair. "You may not be too ignorant to learn a few things. But do not interrupt. Listen. Too many questions, and I end the lesson."

"Of course," Jacquelyn agreed.

And she sat fascinated for an hour, while the shopkeeper pointed to item after item and told her of its history. Jacquelyn had thought herself knowledgeable, but she realized there was more to learn about periods, craftsmanship and the background of antiques than one could possibly absorb in a lifetime.

Jacquelyn left the shop feeling both enlightened and humbled. The shopkeeper had a way of making her feel stupid for not knowing more about the world of antiques. If she had more time to spend in his company, she would acquire a broad knowledge.

While there, Jacquelyn had settled on an Empire acajou Table-Gueridon. Its three legs were connected by a triangular piece that supported the decorative figures standing proudly under the edge of the table. It was in excellent condition, and the price seemed fair in light of the history the shopkeeper had told her about it.

Jacquelyn considered the possibility that the spritely shopkeeper had pulled a fast one on her. But she had examined the table closely, looking for signs of fake wear put there by hands experienced at reproducing old masters. She found none of those. She had checked the underside of the table to determine if the wood had been stained. It had not, which was another sign of authenticity. It sometimes took a sharp eye to detect a fake.

Jacquelyn spent the rest of the morning browsing in other antique shops. She found some fascinating mirrors and a chandelier or two, but nothing she thought truly suitable for Cypress Halls.

As agreed, Jacquelyn met Scott at the café he had

designated for lunch. She stood self-consciously on the sidewalk, waiting for him, not sure whether to take a seat at one of the tables under the bright green umbrellas.

Then she saw a shock of unruly brown hair advancing toward her. The sun glinted down on the pair of brown horn-rimmed sunglasses Scott wore. She was surprised at how relieved she felt to see a familiar face—even Scott McCrann's.

When he reached her, he took her elbow. "Hungry?" he asked, smiling down at her, standing so close she could almost hear his heartbeat. From the corner of her eye she saw a couple at one of the tables, holding hands.

"Yes," she answered.

Scott led her to a table and pulled out a cane chair. He popped up the green umbrella to provide some shade and took a seat opposite her.

A waiter with a white cloth thrown over his left arm approached the table.

"What will you have?" Scott asked Jacquelyn.

"I don't know. Everything looks and smells so good." She saw waiters serving plates with small whole fish, fancy-looking pastries and bright, crisp vegetables. Tart, vinegary aromas blended with the heavy smells of cream sauces.

"You decide," Jacquelyn suggested.

Scott turned to the waiter, gave the order in French and then leaned on the small round table with his elbows.

"Did you find anything this morning?" Scott asked.

"Yes," Jacquelyn said. "But it's rather discouraging. I can see how long it's going to take to find what

I really want. I could stay here a year and not have an opportunity to see everything I might be interested in."

"Then I have good news for you," Scott said.

"What?" Jacquelyn asked.

Instead of answering, Scott nodded to call her attention to someone behind her. She turned and saw an overweight man with a large red Piermaria accordian strapped to his shoulders. The man's round face had an expectant look. Scott nodded. The musician's fingers danced over the keyboard as he pumped the bellows back and forth. The spritely strains of a popular French tune made Jacquelyn momentarily forget her conversation with Scott.

She swayed in time to the music. Customers at nearby tables turned to watch the performance.

When the musician had finished, Scott pressed some bills into his hands.

"Merci, monsieur," he said.

"That was delightful," Jacquelyn cried, applauding the man.

He bowed slightly from the waist, *"Merci, mam'selle."* He stepped back as the waiter placed their plates on the table.

"Oh, that looks good," Jacquelyn exclaimed, her mouth watering. "What is it?"

"It is beef *à la ficelle* boiled with vegetables. These are scalloped potatoes. And that is liver pâté."

The dark meat evoked a rapturous response from Jacquelyn's taste buds. She hadn't realized how hungry she was.

"It's delicious," she said, rolling her eyes in appreciation.

"All food in France is delicious," Scott smiled. "The French take their greatest pride in their cooking. It's rather like New Orleans. It's hard to get a bad meal here."

"You really love this country, don't you?" Jacquelyn asked, touched by the depth with which Scott understood France. She pierced a potato with her fork.

"Yes, I do," Scott said. He paused in his eating. "Paris is the city of romance. It casts a spell over all who visit. Someday I plan to set up a residence here and spend part of my time living the French life. That's why I am here now, to make preliminary plans to open a branch office soon."

"You mean you're going to divide your time between the United States and France?" Jacquelyn asked.

"Something like that," Scott said.

"That sounds marvelous," Jacquelyn said. "I wish I had a chance to do that."

"You could have," Scott murmured, bitterness tingeing his voice. He cast her a meaningful glance.

Jacquelyn's hand, raising a fork to her lips, paused in midair. Suddenly, the sumptuous French lunch had lost its flavor.

"What was the good news you mentioned a while ago?" she asked abruptly, changing the subject. If anyone knew how to rub it in, it was Scott, Jacquelyn thought grimly. Leave it to him to remind her that had she become Mrs. Scott McCrann, she would be here today as his wife rather than as an interior decorator. And she would be looking forward to frequent trips to Paris with him.

Scott's hard expression seemed frozen for an instant. Then his features relaxed. "I think you may have a chance to find quite a few of the decorating items you need without having to spend so much time looking in small shops. I heard today at my business meeting about an estate sale not far from Paris. An old home, formerly owned by an aristocratic family, has fallen into the hands of a Swiss family. They are selling off a lot of the furnishings, all of them French, and plan to redecorate in a different motif. Tomorrow there will be private showings for a small, select group of prospective buyers. Are you interested?"

"Interested?" Jacquelyn exclaimed. "Of course I'm interested. But will I be allowed in?"

"No," Scott said slowly, his eyes sparkling with mischief. "But I will. And you can come along as my assistant."

Jacquelyn felt a tingle of excitement. She dug into the rest of her lunch with relish. Suddenly the day took on a fresh sparkle. There was nothing like the anticipation of a new antique treasure to give life zest—unless it was the magic of love. But it was too late for that with Scott. She would never again know the closeness of his arms, the warmth of his bare hands on her back as he rubbed suntan lotion on her. She would never again feel the pleasure of his mouth on hers in a passionate kiss. Even in Paris, the city of lovers, their estrangement was too deep and permanent to salvage even a shred of their former feelings for each other.

They finished their lunch, exchanging small talk about the possible antiques Jacquelyn might find. She rambled on about the table she had located in the first antique shop and asked Scott about having it shipped back home. He assured her she could have anything she thought appropriate sent back to the States and promised to take care of it.

"That is, if I approve of the purchase," Scott added.

"Of course," Jacquelyn said, holding onto her temper with an effort.

They returned to the hotel after lunch to rest. Jacquelyn stretched out on the big bed, closed her eyes and drifted off to sleep.

When she woke up, Natalie was standing beside the bed.

"Did you enjoy having Scott all to yourself today?" she asked, her dark eyes burning with resentment. She sat on the deep burgundy velvet bedspread of the other bed and ran a long fingernail down the pile.

Jacquelyn pushed herself to a sitting position.

"Oh, Natalie," she said, "you know it was strictly business."

"Was it? What did you and Scott talk about?"

"Antiques, of course!" Jacquelyn shot back. "What else?" She was in no mood to cope with Natalie's jealousy.

"I don't believe you," Natalie said.

Jacquelyn swung her legs off the bed. She ran her stocking feet back and forth across the plush carpet. The sensation helped soothe her so she could stay in control of her emotions. "Scott spent most of the morning at a business meeting."

Natalie's eyes reflected her disbelief. Then she said, "Austin wants you to go with him tonight. Scott is taking me to Maxim's for dinner. Just the two of us."

The intent of her words was quite clear and the barrier between Jacquelyn and Natalie grew wider.

Jacquelyn knew she contributed in part to the

reserve she felt around her childhood friend. But she was tired of being put on the defensive about Scott.

She decided the best offensive tactic was to quit apologizing to Natalie. The girl was bound to think the worst, anyway.

Impulsively, Jacquelyn reached out and took Natalie's hand in hers. "Natalie, this jealousy is so silly. There is nothing between Scott and me."

"I know," Natalie said firmly, extracting her hand from Jacquelyn's grasp. "But that doesn't stop Scott from wanting to have you just the same, only to satisfy his male pride. And it doesn't prevent you from falling victim to his charms again. I know how disarming he can be when he tries. He could turn any woman's head, even yours. Watch yourself, Jacquelyn. This trip is not just a shopping expedition."

"What do you mean by that?" Jacquelyn asked.

"I know Scott better than you think. I know what he has on his mind. I ought to hate him for what he's trying to do. But I can't. I just feel sorry for you."

Jacquelyn frowned. "Well, you needn't," she replied sharply. "I can take care of myself."

It was irritating that everyone seemed to think her so helpless. First Scott acted as if the devil himself might carry her off when he let her out on rue Bonaparte to go shopping. Now Natalie seemed to think Jacquelyn incapable of seeing through Scott's suave ruse. She was perfectly capable of looking out for her own interests.

That night, after Natalie and Scott had left on their date, Austin stopped by the hotel room to pick up Jacquelyn. She was in a reckless, defiant mood. She had pulled out her most glamorous dress. It was a white wraparound silk fabric that clung to her curves and gave her a voluptuous appearance. Its thin spaghetti straps ran over smooth, well-shaped shoulders and down a slender back to a low-cut scoop that showed off Jacquelyn's supple skin to advantage.

She piled her hair high on her head, knotting it into a sophisticated bun with little wisps of hair dangling seductively in front of each ear. She lined her eyes with eyebrow pencil, making them look even larger, and last, she flicked mascara on the ends of her lashes.

She'd show Natalie, she thought. No more playing the demure mouse around either Scott or Austin. She was in Paris, the city of romance and love, and she was determined to enjoy herself.

Austin took one look at Jacquelyn and his eyes widened.

"Jacquelyn, you look beautiful," he gasped. His gaze trailed from her head down to her shoes. "All this, for me?" he asked.

"Sure," Jacquelyn said, laughing. "Why not?" In truth, she thought, it was actually for herself.

Austin was captivated by Jacquelyn's appearance. He took her hand and led her down the corridor of the hotel. When they emerged onto the street he kept his eyes on her.

A gentle breeze tossed Jacquelyn's tendrils of hair around her face, giving her a carefree, abandoned quality. The night lights of the city sparkled. Jacquelyn felt more daring and alive than she ever had in her life. She eyed lovers huddled in corners, kissing in the dim light, and let Austin squeeze her hand tighter.

As they strolled down the sidewalk, they came upon a small woman selling tulips from a brightly colored cart. On a platform built into the cart she had spread out a dinner of bread and cheese. She uncorked a bottle of wine, carefully poured herself a drink and sipped the liquid slowly, obviously savoring its flavor.

Austin stopped at the stand, motioned to an assortment of red flowers and paid the woman. He handed the bouquet to Jacquelyn and slipped his arm around her waist.

She did not pull back. In fact, she leaned in closer to him. Why shouldn't she enjoy his closeness? she thought. She had spent so much of her life restraining her emotions.

She had never let Scott know how deeply hurt she was at the way he had treated her brother, Gerrard. She had never told Austin how truly fond of him she was, in spite of the fact that she could never love him in a romantic way. She had never explained to Uncle Luther how crushed she had been when her relationship with Scott had ended. She had tried to smoothe over the kissing incident in the garden with Scott to spare Natalie's feelings.

But now she was tired of worrying about other people. She was alive and well in the city of lovers—Paris, France—and the mood of the country was penetrating her shield. She wanted to feel the thrill of romance, to experience the gaiety all around her. What harm was there in that? she thought. Austin knew she didn't love him, so why shouldn't she let him hold her hand and put his arm around her? It was friendship, nothing more, and they both knew it. That's all they could ever feel for each other.

For the moment, Jacquelyn was in love with love, and the partner in her escape into fantasy was less important than the emotion carrying her on its cascading rush of excitement.

Why shouldn't she give herself over to the magic of Paris just for now? she thought. She would probably never come here again, and no one who stepped on Parisian soil should be denied the ecstasy of this city's kiss.

Austin and Jacquelyn strolled slowly by the shop fronts. A street vendor near a sidewalk café offered them pastries. Jacquelyn nodded, held the thin-shelled morsel to her mouth and bit in. The succulent, sugary center melted and oozed across her tongue, making her taste buds prickle with delight. A delightful sensation rippled through her. Never had anything tasted so delicious.

Somewhere in the distance, a cat meowed. A horse pulling a wagon clopped by. A man selling red, white and blue balloons on the corner sang out for customers to buy his wares.

It was a night of enchantment, and Jacquelyn wanted it to last forever.

She and Austin took a night ride in a boat on the Seine. As they cruised along, Jacquelyn's eyes sparkled in the dim light. She and Austin talked softly about the sights. At one point, the green vegetation trailing down the wall of the bank almost covered the brick barrier. It was beautiful.

Later, they found themselves at the foot of the Eiffel Tower, holding hands as the golden water sprayed forth from the ground-level fountains. They stood near enough to catch the soft, cool spray of fine mist blowing in the breeze.

"Jacquelyn," said Austin huskily. "I've never seen you like this."

"I've never felt like this," she said. She was on a different plain of consciousness from any she had ever experienced before. She had been transported to a realm beyond the reality of the moment, to a neverland of anticipation and delight a thousand miles away from the everyday mundane world.

"I know what it is," Austin said softly, his mouth close to her ear.

"Yes. I do, too," Jacquelyn agreed.

"It's love, Jacquelyn," Austin said, his voice thick with emotion.

"Then you feel it, too?" Jacquelyn asked. She didn't know whether a man could be carried away by the splendor and rapture of Paris. A separate part of her was vaguely aware of the direction the conversation was heading, but she was too elated to care.

"Yes, I feel it, too," Austin said, pulling Jacquelyn close to him. "Jacquelyn, this is the perfect place to ask you. You know how I feel about you. It's taken you a long time to return those feelings, but I sense something different in you tonight. Is the time right? Have you fallen in love with me?"

Jacquelyn heard the question, but she couldn't answer. She was someone new tonight, a caterpillar who had just emerged from its cocoon, and she wasn't sure of her old self. Had she really cared more for Austin than she had thought? Was that why she had been swept along on the tide of a new rush of feelings? Or was it the intrigue of Paris that had her under its spell?

"I—I don't know, Austin," Jacquelyn confessed. "I feel so different. I don't know what it is. I don't seem to be myself at all."

"Maybe this is the real you," Austin said. "You've

hidden behind such a wall of reserve. Perhaps it took coming to Paris for you to find yourself."

"Perhaps," Jacquelyn said vaguely. "I just don't know."

"Jacquelyn," Austin said seriously, "will you marry me?"

"Marry you?" Jacquelyn asked. She heard the question, but it made no impact on her. She looked at Austin, at his dark hair and eyes, at his good looks. But she felt nothing. Everything else seemed so right. The city was perfect, the time was ripe, the atmosphere was romantic. The ambience suggested love everywhere they looked. But something was missing. What was it?

"Yes, Jacquelyn, will you marry me?" Austin lifted one of her hands and brought her fingers to his lips.

Suddenly, confusion washed over her and extinguished some of the heavenly glow she had felt.

"Austin, I just don't know," Jacquelyn answered slowly. "I'm trying to be as honest as I can. You know I'm fond of you. You're the best friend I have. But I'm not sure I love you or will ever love you. Maybe it's just the night, the beauty of the city, the atmosphere."

"No," Austin assured her. "It's none of those. It's love Jacquelyn. I know it is. You love me. You're just afraid to admit it."

Jacquelyn looked blankly at Austin. Her heart had stopped beating. A tingle of fear gripped her. Was he right?

Chapter Seven

"Yes, my neart belongs to you," Jacquelyn whispered hoarsely. But it was not to Austin she was talking. Instead, she spoke to the city of love as she and Scott sped along in the car he had leased for the day.

Last night she had not been sure of her feelings. Too much confusion from the suddenness of the change in her had left her bewildered. But today, back out in the street once more, she knew. It had not been Austin that had captured her heart, it had been Paris.

Just as she had resisted giving in so many times before—when Scott had wanted her to marry him before she had had her growing up time in New Orleans, when Uncle Luther had wanted her to restore the mansion—she had resisted again. This time, it had been to the allure of Paris.

Jacquelyn had been so brokenhearted after her

breakup with Scott that she didn't want to allow herself any romantic feelings ever again. That's why she had been reluctant to see the tourist attractions. She had wanted to remain in her protective shell. But her encounter with Natalie had unleashed a side of her she hadn't realized existed any longer. It had freed her to be herself again, to relish the appeal of the sights, sounds, tastes and atmosphere of the world's most divine city.

She didn't know how Scott had arranged for just the two of them to drive to the estate sale, but she was beyond caring.

"Make sure you're back in time for the four of us to go to the Moulin Rouge," Natalie had ordered just before Jacquelyn had left that morning.

"We'll try," Jacquelyn tossed off casually. It was the first time she hadn't cared whether Natalie got mad or not. Jacquelyn was no longer afraid of her childhood chum and wondered why she had ever been a coward around her in the first place. What kind of power had Natalie exerted over her?

At first Jacquelyn had been upset over their spat. But now she was grateful it had taken place. Only after Natalie had succeeded in killing some of Jacquelyn's concern for her feelings was Jacquelyn able to assert herself.

The car slowed at an intersection. Scott stopped. They sat there a long time.

"What's the matter?" Jacquelyn asked.

"Traffic jam." Scott chuckled. "The man at the rental agency warned me about the overload of automobiles in Paris."

"Just another of the charms of Paris," Jacquelyn quipped.

"You don't mind being tied up here for who knows how long?"

"Not if you don't."

"Then we might as well enjoy it." Scott smiled.

"What do you mean?"

"You'll see."

Scott opened the door, hopped out of the car and strode to the rear. He lifted the hatchback, took out a basket and returned. Jacquelyn noticed other motorists getting out of their vehicles and taking various items from the backseat or from the trunk.

As Scott climbed back in, Jacquelyn couldn't help noticing the glint of the sun on his brown hair. His hand, with its lean, strong fingers, placed the tan wicker basket between them on the seat. He lifted the lid and extracted a bottle of wine and two glasses. He reached in for a small chunk of cheese and a stack of crackers.

"A snack . . . here?" Jacquelyn asked.

"Why not? We may be here quite a while. We might as well enjoy ourselves."

Jacquelyn laughed softly. "Sure, why not?" she agreed. She settled back in the seat, a comfortable, relaxed feeling stealing over her. As Scott poured them each a drink, she let her eyes wander in the direction of the street. The door of one car, which was bumper-to-bumper with another vehicle, flew open, and a wiry man in a beret leaped out. He strode menacingly over to his mechanical opponent and kicked the front tire with a vengeance. The driver of the assaulted automobile waved a clenched fist out the window and drew himself half out of the opening, hurling a barrage of French insults at his assailant.

"The French are a very emotional people, aren't

they?" Jacquelyn observed, taking the glass Scott offered her.

"Like everybody else, some are, some aren't," Scott said. "But the atmosphere here is one of less reserve. The people are freer to express their feelings openly. They are less likely to hide behind a veneer of restraint. That's one of the things I like about Paris. I can be more myself here."

Jacquelyn nibbled the cheese and digested Scott's comment. "How do you mean?" she asked. She set her glass on the basket, which Scott had now closed.

"It's the ambience of the city," Scott explained. "At home in the United States, there's more of a requirement to be in control of one's emotions. I guess it comes from our Puritan heritage. Men are ashamed to cry. They don't hug in public and oftentimes not even in their families. We deny so many of our feelings. We try to talk people out of grief, sadness, anger and hostility. When our children are hurt, instead of acknowledging their pain, we tell them not to cry, to be brave.

"But here in Paris, emotional responses are expected. If a man is angry, he can wave his fists and shout. No one expects him to bottle up his feelings and pretend they don't exist. If someone is grieved, his friends cry with him instead of trying to cheer him up. The French are not afraid of their emotions."

Jacquelyn was touched by the tone of Scott's voice. She had never heard him talk like this before. It was as if she had been introduced to a new dimension of his character. She had thought him capable only of ruthlessness and a selfish desire to satisfy his own wants. Even though she had once loved him, she had not known this side of his nature.

Maybe that was part of the reason she had been willing to spend a year in New Orleans away from him.

She must have sensed there was something lacking. Now she realized he was much deeper and more complex than she had thought. He had possessed a warmth she had never known. It must have always been there, but he had kept it tightly under wraps, like a mummy in a deep, mysterious tomb. She had sensed there was more to Scott, but she had never been able to penetrate the facade and get to the real man.

Today, Jacquelyn was glimpsing the eternal depths of Scott she had never seen before. A little ripple of fear shot through her. There was something dangerous in the way he was exposing his inner nature to her.

"Don't you sense it, Jacquelyn?" Scott asked. "The magic appeal of this town? Just look out there now. Men are free to kick tires, hurl insults and shout away their frustrations from being tied up in this snarl of traffic. In America, if motorists stalled in freeway traffic did the same thing, just imagine how many ulcers could be prevented!" Scott laughed freely, the sound reverberating in the little car like a deep-pitched bell.

Jacquelyn noticed how much softer the lines around Scott's mouth had become. The hard glint in his eyes was now a twinkle. His strong, masculine hands dwarfed the glass goblet he held. For this moment, Scott McCrann seemed larger than life, a man who grabbed fate by the throat and made it bend to his will. Yet he was a man who flowed freely with the river of life, willingly molding himself to the ups and downs of existence, but always maintaining the upper hand in the game of living. Jacquelyn sensed a power in Scott she had not recognized before, and she felt a driving need to find out more about this man she had thought she knew. It was as if she were meeting him for the first time, and she was fascinated.

But before she could ask him more, he reached toward the ignition and twisted the keys.

"Looks like we can be on our way," he said, starting the engine. He lifted the lid on the basket, dropped in the cheese and crackers and reached for her glass. She shook her head, indicating she did not want the wine. Scott downed it and put both glasses to rest side by side in the basket. Jacquelyn noticed how close they lay together, their rims touching. Would they be broken by their close proximity? Why did the glasses remind her of Scott and herself?

The car eased forward and Jacquelyn sat back against the seat. She sighed. She had been in the grips of a lovely, enchanted spell. Why couldn't it have lasted longer?

The rest of the conversation seemed trivial compared to the flash of truth Jacquelyn had experienced with Scott. They chatted easily now, the former hostility temporarily washed away by the glamour of Paris.

As they made their way out of the inner city and toward the small village Scott had told her about, Jacquelyn realized how different Scott seemed here in this other part of the world. Was it really that Scott was different, or was it that she was different? Or had the charms of Paris transformed them both into two new people who were meeting each other for the first time?

Jacquelyn knew she felt different. Ever since

yesterday, when she had finally succumbed to the charisma of this foreign atmosphere, she had floated along with an abandoned, devil-may-care headiness. She had shown it again this morning when she dressed. She had pulled all her hair over to one side and caught it up in a decorative clip. It cascaded down over her right shoulder and lent her a French air, which she adored. She had slipped into a bright yellow low-cut sundress with daring little cutouts in the back. The hem snapped around her legs as she walked in her high-heeled sandals. Today, just for fun, she had placed an artificial mole by her lower left lip. She had primped in the mirror, tossing her hair back over her shoulder and laughing, before she had wiped the fake beauty mark away.

Jacquelyn *was* different. But what about Scott? Was he transformed too? Or did he just seem that way because she was changed?

Well, she thought lazily. It didn't matter. Nothing mattered right now but this moment, this feeling. She didn't know how long it was going to last, but she was going to absorb it completely into her being and enjoy it to the fullest.

She recalled with pleasure Scott's face when he had seen her that morning. She had always been a little on the conservative side. But her appearance today shouted how quickly she had thrown off the ordinary constraints. Scott's eyes had sparkled with an approving glow. His mouth had curved into a smile. His touch had been warm, close, intimate.

An almost wicked feeling had gripped Jacquelyn when she noted the obvious anger in Natalie's eyes as Scott escorted Jacquelyn down the corridor from their hotel room. Normally, she would have been disturbed by this type of incident. But today she relished the look on Natalie's face. It gave her some kind of perverse pleasure to have the upper hand for a change.

Jacquelyn felt herself absorbing the defiant, self-indulgent behavior of the typical Parisian. For now she understood with a new depth their rebellious nature. Life was a vibrant, pulsating heart, and she had become a part of it. She wanted to taste its nectar, to savor its flavor, to experience its joys and sorrows. To do that, she had to give herself over to her emotions, to allow herself to give vent to the full range of her impulses. She must hold nothing back.

Reddish brown rooftops came into view as Jacquelyn looked out the car window. The high-peaked buildings were dotted with skylights and gables. Nestled closely, with small groves of trees sprouting up here and there, they looked like some small village Jacquelyn had seen in a travel picture book as a child.

Scott turned off before they entered the heart of the small town and drove along a narrow paved road lined on both sides with towering trees. The sunlight flashed brightly through the trees as the car cruised slowly toward a huge white mansion.

"This looks like the right place," Scott said, indicating the three-story structure with large colon-nades. He checked a slip of paper that bore directions.

"Oh, Scott, it looks divine," Jacquelyn gasped. "And very expensive. It reminds me of Cypress Halls."

Scott nodded. "I have a feeling we're going to find exactly what you're looking for here."

"Do you really think so?" she asked, excitement mounting.

"Let's find out." Scott pulled the car to a stop several yards from the front door. The circular drive was dotted with vehicles. An elegant woman with steel gray hair, granny glasses and a smart blue suit emerged from the front door.

"Looks like they have some customers already, Jacquelyn said, frowning. "I hope we haven't missed all the good buys."

"In a house this size, I think there will be plenty to go around." Scott chuckled. "After all, we don't need to furnish the whole of Cypress Halls."

"Yes, I guess I'm just excited. I have a good feeling about this place, Scott." Suddenly, Jacquelyn realized she had called Scott by his first name. She blushed at how easily the word had flowed from her lips. Until now, she had judiciously avoided calling him anything. She had kept their relationship as impersonal as possible by being as formal as she could.

Scott smiled warmly as he helped Jacquelyn out of the car. When his hand touched hers, she suddenly forgot all about antiques and Cypress Halls. For an instant, all that mattered was the warmth of his skin on hers, the tingle that zipped through her, the breathlessness that left her feeling light-headed.

Silently, they walked the few steps over the graveled drive to the front door. The ground crunched under their feet with a sharp crackle. A cool breeze brushed across Jacquelyn's bare arms. A bird soared noiselessly near the rooftop, landing on the edge of a high peak. It looked down at them and chirped. At the far side of the mansion, a robust man in overalls bent over a row of hedges with a pair of shiny clippers, trimming back the overgrowth.

Scott pushed a button at the side of the massive

wooden front door. In a matter of seconds, the door swung open and a petite woman of about fifty smiled up at them.

She said something in French. Scott answered, and they were ushered inside.

The inside of the house was spectacular. Jacquelyn felt a surge of pride knowing that she was in the process of putting Cypress Halls back into the same kind of condition as this magnificent structure. The woman took them through the rooms containing the items for sale. Jacquelyn ran her hands over smooth wood, fingered the delicate glass and crystal drops on the chandeliers, saw herself reflected in ornate mirrors and sat in chairs lovingly carved by master craftsmen of long ago.

She dallied over fine vases, silver, goblets, clocks, mugs and intricate tapestries.

Jacquelyn found a Louie XV tulipwood parquetry *table de dame*. She ran her fingers over the ornate top and along the smooth wood bordering the design. She let her hands slide in and out along the scalloped edge, marveling at the fine workmanship. It was in superior condition. The intricate carvings at the top of each table leg were as sharp and finely honed as the day they had been fashioned. The slightly curved legs were fluid and graceful.

"I want this," Jacquelyn sighed, looking at Scott, her eyes bright with the excitement of discovery.

"Is that all?" Scott asked.

"Oh, no," Jacquelyn said. "There's more. But I want to take my time. I want to enjoy this moment."

"Go ahead," Scott said. "That's why we're here. Indulge yourself."

Those were the finest words Jacquelyn had heard in a long while. And she took Scott up on his offer.

She wandered around the house, imagining herself living in a time long past, when elegance and manners were the order of the day.

It was with a stab of regret that Jacquelyn finally announced that she was finished. She had found exactly what she needed to complete one wing of the mansion and to fill in the gaps that she knew would exist after she'd browsed some more in New Orleans for the rest of the furniture she wanted. She would have enjoyed more time here, but she knew they had to head back to Paris soon to meet Natalie and Austin for their evening at the Moulin Rouge together.

Scott made the arrangements to pay for Jacquelyn's choices and to have them shipped to the States. While he was taking care of that matter, Jacquelyn was allowed to roam in the other rooms of the estate house.

Finally they were back in the car headed for Paris.

"I would say that was well worth the trip, wouldn't you?" Scott asked.

"Yes," Jacquelyn agreed enthusiastically. "Thank you for making it possible."

"My pleasure."

For a moment, Jacquelyn imagined that the barrier between them had crumbled. She felt as if she and Scott were standing on a grassy meadow, looking across the buttercups and sunflowers, smiling at each other.

Impulsively, Jacquelyn asked, "Scott, what were you like as a child? It's funny, but I never asked you that before. It didn't occur to me, but now I'm curious."

"Why now?" Scott asked, taking his eyes off the road momentarily.

"I don't know. Just the atmosphere here, I guess. It makes me curious about you." Jacquelyn blurted out her answer. It scared her that she could be so honest with a man she didn't trust. But the old feelings of antagonism were melting away. What Scott had done seemed less important now than it had then.

"I guess I was about average," Scott said.

"Average? You?" Jacquelyn asked incredulously, laughing. "There's not an average bone in your body. What was your mother like?"

"I don't know," Scott answered, his voice sounding strained. "She deserted my father when I was only five."

"Oh, Scott, I'm sorry. You never told me."

"You never asked," he said.

It was true, she realized. She had been so wrapped up in her love affair with Scott that all she had been able to think about was the moment. Had she been in love with love? It had never occurred to her that she might get clues to his personality if she knew more about his background. It hadn't seemed important in those intoxicating days of romantic fulfillment.

Scott suddenly muttered something and pumped the accelerator.

"What's the matter?" she asked.

"I don't know. The car is missing."

Sputtering noises growled in the engine and the car began to jerk unevenly.

Jacquelyn looked out the window. Down the road, she saw a cluster of quaint French buildings. "Do you think we can make it as far as there?" she asked, pointing to the structures.

"I don't know," Scott said, fiddling with the switch, his foot still pumping the gas pedal.

The car began to slow again, this time coasting for longer and longer periods of time before it jumped back into life. Finally, it coasted one last time and came to a gentle halt several hundred yards from the buildings.

"Do you mind walking?" Scott asked.

"Not at all," Jacquelyn said, slipping out of her heels. "But I think I'll go barefoot, if you don't mind. Please turn your head."

Scott frowned, looking puzzled.

"My hose," she explained. "If I don't take them off, I'll ruin them. And if you don't look in the other direction, I'll embarrass myself."

"Oh?" Scott said, a teasing grin on his face. "I've seen your legs before. Don't forget all the times you've worn a bathing suit around me."

"It's not the same thing," Jacquelyn protested with mock indignation, "and you know it."

"Yeah," Scott growled seductively.

"Scott McCrann!" Jacquelyn exclaimed.

"Okay, okay," Scott said with a chuckle. "If it saves your modesty, I won't look, I promise."

With a broad sweep of his arms, he placed his hands over his eyes like a kid playing hide-and-seek.

"Now, go ahead."

Jacquelyn eyed him suspiciously, lifted her skirt and slipped down her hose. Scott parted his fingers mischievously, peeked through the opening and gave a low whistle.

"You promised!" she said.

"I promised I wouldn't look. I didn't promise I wouldn't peek."

"That's not fair," Jacquelyn said vehemently, pushing his hands back before his eyes.

"Why not?" Scott asked huskily, taking his hands down. He turned in the seat to look at her. Suddenly the game turned into a duel. Their eyes met and clashed, each seeking to control the situation by sheer force of will. An electric current shot through Jacquelyn. The frivolity had become a probe. Scott's blue eyes searched Jacquelyn's face. But their intensity penetrated deeper into her being, locking into her eyes and silently questioning her.

What was it Scott wanted to know? For an instant, it didn't matter what the question was. Jacquelyn was flying on a magic carpet of emotion, and no matter what he asked, the answer would be yes. She wanted nothing more than to grant any request he would make of her. Her heart had stopped in her chest and her blood had halted in her veins. The world stood still on its axis because she felt sure Scott was going to kiss her. Her body ached for his touch. Her soul longed for his embrace. She was caught up in a magic spell of enchantment that she wanted to last forever.

Just then, Jacquelyn heard a tap on the window. She shook her head to clear her vision and she shot a resentful glance in the direction of the intruding sound.

Suddenly, for the first time, Jacquelyn realized it was sprinkling. A fine mist enshrouded a man's face at the window of the car. He held a black umbrella over his head and tapped once again on the window-pane.

Scott turned, rolled down the window and spoke to the man in French.

Jacquelyn sat silently. But inside, her thoughts were a jumble of confused feelings. What had just transpired between her and Scott? What did it mean? Why did she feel so frustrated, so agitated, so edgy? What had France done to her? It couldn't be real, what she was experiencing. She had allowed herself to become a victim of the romance of Paris, and she had become confused by her own responses. She was going to have to get a grip on herself. The first thing she did was reach up and remove the clip from her hair, letting it fall loosely down her back.

"He saw us stall along the road," Scott explained, pointing to the smiling face peering in the car window. "He has a little restaurant down the road. We can get something to eat there and call for another car."

"Fine," Jacquelyn answered. "I'm getting awfully hungry." But it was more than just food that she craved. It was a hunger of the soul, a hunger she didn't understand or know how to satisfy.

They hopped out of the car and huddled under the umbrella together. A fine spray scattered over them as they walked down the side of the road. Jacquelyn carried her purse in one hand. The rough road scraped the soles of her feet.

"Want me to carry you?" Scott asked.

"No," Jacquelyn answered sharply, then wondered why her tone had been so abrupt.

The inside of the café was cozy and intimate. A small light in the center of the room illuminated the handful of tables with their crisp white tablecloths. A counter ran across the back of the room. Wine bottles sat in a rack to one side of the cash register.

The proprietor of the café folded his umbrella, shook off the pools of water and set it in a stand near the door.

There was one other couple in the restaurant. A young man and an attractive woman sat huddled over a small table with a single candle in the center. They leaned toward each other and held hands. Jacquelyn felt a warm glow start somewhere in the region of her heart and radiate out through her body, carrying with it an intense longing. Was it simply hunger?

Scott led Jacquelyn to a table and pulled out a chair for her to sit down. He took the one opposite her.

The owner scurried back to the kitchen and began talking in a loud voice. Soon he reappeared at the table, spoke to Scott in French and stood with an expectant expression on his face.

"Well," Scott said, "looks as if we've made quite a hit with the management. He's offering to let us come to his wine cellar and pick out our own bottle. Interested?"

"Why would he do that?" Jacquelyn asked.

"It must be the rented car. I asked him to phone for a replacement. He obviously assumes we are sufficiently flush to warrant special treatment."

"What would the car have to do with it?"

"He knows we're foreigners and thinks we're rich."

"Well, aren't we?" Jacquelyn asked lightly, momentarily forgetting that she was merely a hired hand as far as Scott was concerned.

"I guess so," Scott agreed amiably. "Now, how about the wine cellar? Do you want to see it?"

"Sure, I'd love it. I've never been in a French wine

cellar. Who could turn down a new adventure like that?"

Scott nodded to the man and pulled Jacquelyn's chair out for her. They followed the café owner to the back of the room and through a narrow door. They descended steep steps into a dank plastered room.

The man pushed a button on the stairs to illuminate a small light that flickered uneasily. When he reached the floor, he grabbed an overhead cord that switched on a small, bare bulb which gave off a faint light.

The cellar, lined with bloated barrels and bottles stacked in racks on their sides, smelled of fermented corks. The café owner indicated with a sweep of his hand his pride in his fine homemade wines. He spoke to Scott in French, they exchanged comments, and the man reached for a bottle from the rack.

"He's quite proud of his stock," Scott explained. "He's opening us one of the best vintages he owns."

Reaching into his pocket, the man withdrew a small box of matches to light a candle sitting on the top of a wine barrel. When the light flickered into life, the man's face became solemn. He held the candle behind the amber wine bottle. Slowly, he turned the bottle round and round and moved it back and forth in front of the flame.

"He's checking for dregs," Scott said. "The French are very fussy about their wines. It would be an insult if he served us less than his best."

With a satisfied smile, the little man uncorked the bottle, poured a small amount of the liquid into a goblet sitting on the end of another barrel and sniffed the glass. Then he brought the rim of the glass to his lips, slowly sipped the wine and stood for a moment with a thoughtful look on his face.

Jacquelyn stood expectantly. Would he approve of it? When his face broke into a broad smile, she felt a sense of relief. What a shame, she thought, if he had been disappointed in his own product.

When Scott had been poured a sample and had given his smiling nod of approval, they returned to their table with the café owner and the bottle of wine.

Scott ordered their meal from a limited selection of gourmet dishes. Scott chose stuffed shoulder of lamb while Jacquelyn wanted crab soufflé.

They sat waiting for their meal, a candle flickering on the table between them, lending the small room a soft cozy glow.

"Will it take long?" Jacquelyn asked, trying to make small talk.

"Does it matter?" Scott asked. "We can't go anywhere until the car rental service either gets our vehicle repaired or delivers us a replacement. So we might as well enjoy our wait." He picked up his wineglass and nodded toward her. "A toast?"

Jacquelyn smiled. She lifted her glass to his.

"To good times and a beautiful woman," Scott said, his blue eyes lingering on her face.

"Should I say thank you?" Jacquelyn asked, taking only the barest sip of her wine.

"Not to me," Scott answered. "I didn't make you so lovely. I just appreciate what nature created."

"Thank you," Jacquelyn responded demurely. Could that warm feeling in her cheeks be a blush? she wondered. She cast her eyes downward, feeling strangely shy.

"Don't you like the wine?" Scott asked, obviously noticing how little she consumed.

"Oh, it's not that," Jacquelyn explained. "It's just that I've felt so . . . giddy lately, I guess you'd call it, that I don't want to do anything to destroy it. The wine might—" She stopped herself. She hadn't intended to let Scott know how high she had been feeling since yesterday. It was her secret, yet she found herself willingly sharing it with him before she realized what she was saying.

"Then you've felt it, too?" he asked, moving the candle to one side and reaching for her hand.

His warm skin touched hers. A flush spread through her. She tingled all over as his fingers held hers in an intimate embrace. She felt the room grow smaller, and only the two of them existed in time and space, suspended by a thin thread that linked them to reality.

"Yes, I've felt it, but I don't quite know what it is," Jacquelyn murmured.

Just then, the little man approached them with two salads, which he placed on the table. Jacquelyn and Scott had to break their manual contact. Her hand felt cold where it had been warm. Her heart felt empty where it had been full.

Jacquelyn looked at the green and red salad. Suddenly, she knew food was not the answer to the void inside her. She hardly tasted the crisp lettuce as she munched it. All she could experience was the ache inside her, the longing for something she had never felt so intensely before. What kind of magic had Paris wrought that it could turn her emotions upside down like this and leave her feeling this way?

She looked across the table at Scott. The candle-light flickered softly against his face, giving him a mysterious quality. She realized that this man was both friend and stranger. She knew him, yet she had never really known him at all. And that was part of the restlessness she felt, she realized. Something was urging her to get to know Scott.

"You never did finish telling me about your mother," Jacquelyn said.

Scott put down his wineglass. The blue eyes registered pain. Jacquelyn was suddenly sorry she had asked.

"I told you all there was to say," he replied woodenly. "I never really knew my mother."

"Then your father raised you alone?" Jacquelyn ventured.

"No, there was a series of housekeepers who kept an eye on me. One I remember especially. She was young and beautiful, like you. She used to play baseball with me. She could run like the wind. But sometimes, when we raced, she would pretend to stumble so I could beat her. She taught me how to love, and I said I was going to marry her when I grew up. She always took me seriously. She never laughed at me. But she said she was much too old for me. She seemed genuinely sorry about that."

"What happened to her?" Jacquelyn asked.

"One day when I came home from school, she was gone. She deserted me, just like that. She never even said good-bye. My father said she had been offered a job in the city." Scott's voice was hollow, with a quality that failed to mask the hurt.

"That must have been tough," Jacquelyn said, swallowing hard to hold back a tear that threatened to spill over her lids.

"I vowed then and there never to fall in love again," Scott said. His jawline turned hard. His voice was steely. "And then I met you," he said softly.

"And?" Jacquelyn asked, her heart pounding so loudly she wasn't sure she could hear his answer.

Scott was silent for a moment. His hand gripped the wineglass. The veins stood out, throbbing and deep blue. "And you left me for the big city, too," he said in a monotone.

"Oh, Scott," Jacquelyn whispered softly. "I didn't know. Why didn't you tell me?"

Scott shrugged. "It wouldn't have made any difference. It would have sounded childish—silly—not the sort of thing a grown man goes around talking about."

"Oh, but that's not true, Scott," Jacquelyn protested. "A man can tell the secrets of his heart to someone he . . . cares about." Her lips refused to form the words "loves," which was what she really wanted to say. But that had been so long ago, and this was now.

The conversation ended when the café owner approached their table with their entrée. His appearance broke the spell they had been under. It had been an intimate moment, one that comes only seldom, one that cannot be planned in advance. Something in the events of the day had broken down Scott's defenses and had led him to tell her personal memories he had never before revealed. It was as if she had seen a new side of him for the first time. What she had glimpsed was genuine, the real depths of Scott McCrann. And she was troubled that she had responded so openly and wholeheartedly to a man she had learned to hate. Where was that hate now? Why could she not recall it, savor it and feed

on it to protect herself from the feelings of sympathy
he had stirred in her?

It was an hour later when the substitute car was
delivered, and Scott and Jacquelyn drove back to
Paris. Their conversation was casual on the surface,
but there was an undercurrent that had not existed
before, a new feeling of closeness that both of them
tried to pretend did not exist. But it was there, and
Jacquelyn did not want to let go of it.

When they reached the hotel, it was past time for
them to go with Austin and Natalie to the Moulin
Rouge. Scott walked Jacquelyn to her door. There
was a note taped to the door that Natalie and Austin
had gone ahead and Scott and Jacquelyn were to
come on to the club.

"Shall we go?" Jacquelyn asked Scott, handing
him the note. She knew what his answer would be.

"No," he said. "May I come in?"

Jacquelyn didn't answer him. Instead, she handed
him her key.

Inside, Jacquelyn stood nervously looking at
Scott. She didn't understand what was happening,
but she felt an intensity building in both of them.
Scott reached out and took her by the hand. He led
her to the window, drew back the drapery and
directed her attention out the window. There in the
distance she could see the city of Paris laid out
before her feet like a sparkling black diamond
aglitter with the glow of a thousand lights trained on
its many facets. The Eiffel Tower in the background
brought back a surge of the romantic feeling she had
been experiencing ever since yesterday.

"I love this city," Scott murmured, slipping his
arm around her shoulders.

"I've grown to love it, too," Jacquelyn said, leaning her head against Scott's firm shoulder, thrilling at her closeness to him.

Scott turned Jacquelyn to face him. He put his hand under her chin, tilting her head up. For a long, agonizing moment he stared at her, his blue eyes awash with a storm of emotions that both captivated her and frightened her.

Then his lips found hers and a thousand sensations exploded in Jacquelyn. It was as if the whole of the last two days came together in a mighty blast. She felt weak and exhilarated at the same time.

Scott pressed his mouth on hers with an intensity that threatened to drive her wild. She returned his kiss, working her lips back and forth eagerly in response. His arms gathered her in and held her close, taking her breath away.

Scott pulled back and then buried his face in her hair.

"Jacquelyn, I've waited so long for this moment," he said, his voice filled with passion. He eased her back gently on the bed, trailing kisses down her neck and arms as he settled down beside her.

He slipped the strap of her dress off her shoulders and she let him. Nothing mattered now except the fulfillment of the intense longing she had endured these last two days, and it was only now that she could admit, even to herself, what it was. Skillfully, Scott began to satisfy her raging need that had propelled her to the brink of insanity, and she submitted herself to his talents, moaning softly with the ecstasy that comes with knowing that the deepest needs of the heart and body will soon be fulfilled.

The sights and sounds and smells of Paris swirled in her mind as she moved in fluid unison with Scott's hands. He knew just what to do and how long to linger.

Then from somewhere, a disturbing knock began to penetrate the bliss. At first Jacquelyn ignored it. The present sensations were too fantastic to be distracted by just any annoyance. But the knock grew stronger and louder until she could no longer dismiss it. She shook her head to clear her mind and realized someone was knocking on her hotel room door.

"Who is it?" Jacquelyn called impatiently.

"It's me, Natalie. Let me in!"

Chapter Eight

"Yes, I'll marry you," Jacquelyn said.

She met Austin's dark-eyed gaze. She was dimly aware of the night sounds and smells of the garden that surrounded them, cloaking the moment in a special kind of solitude. She thought it fitting that she should accept Austin's proposal at last here in the garden of Cypress Halls, where so many important changes in the drama of her life had taken place.

By accepting Austin's proposal, she was drawing closed an important act of that drama, and the central figure of the act—Scott McCrann—was leaving the stage forever. The final scene of that act had taken place in Paris, but it had been so painful she had tried not to think about it until now, when she was back in the United States.

That night in Paris, Natalie had opened the hotel door with her key. By the time she had entered the room, Jacquelyn was off the bed and trying to

154

straighten her dress. Scott had moved over by the window.

Natalie's black eyes had taken in the scene at a glance—the rumpled bed, Jacquelyn's disheveled appearance. She had turned pale as an expression of mingled hurt and anger crossed her face.

Jacquelyn had felt her face grow hot from embarrassment mingled with her own feelings of anger. The atmosphere in the room was charged with tension. For a brittle moment, no one spoke. Then with surprising casualness Scott asked, "Where's Austin?"

Jacquelyn stared at him with disbelief. How could he be so cool under the circumstances?

Without taking her eyes off Jacquelyn, Natalie had drawn a deep breath, touching her tongue to her lips. Then she said, "Austin went to your room looking for you, Scott. We didn't know what had happened—why you didn't show up. We got worried. . . ." Her voice trailed off. She seemed very close to tears.

Jacquelyn watched Scott expectantly. It was his place to clarify this situation. It would be impossible to resume relationships as if nothing had happened. Surely Scott would make his feelings clear, would tell Natalie what had happened tonight, about the passion that had been rekindled between him and Jacquelyn. She couldn't believe that he would simply shrug off the past few hours.

But that was exactly what he did!

"We had car trouble," he said shortly. He strode past the two of them then hesitated at the door. "I'll see if Austin wants to go back to the club."

"No," Natalie murmured. "I don't want to go."

"Neither do I," Jacquelyn said, feeling dazed. A

pain, growing in her chest, cut off any further words. This would have been the proper moment for Scott to make clear his true feelings about her. Not two minutes ago they had been rushing headlong into a raging storm of passion. She had been willing to surrender herself completely to the moment. But now Scott had withdrawn behind a shell of cold reserve. She felt shut out and abandoned as he left, closing the door behind him.

Natalie moved past her. She gazed out the window, her exquisitely beautiful features now chiseled in icy stone. "So Scott won," she murmured sadly, ". . . and we both lost."

"I—I don't know what you mean," Jacquelyn said, though of course, she did.

"Yes you do." Natalie turned. Her wide dark eyes seemed to engulf the room. "I warned you about Scott's intentions, but you wouldn't listen. Or maybe you did listen but thought you could take care of yourself. I knew once Scott combined his masculine charm with this Paris setting you'd be an easy target. He got what he wanted from you, Jacquelyn. He got his revenge. And now he's laughing at you."

"He didn't get anything," Jacquelyn mumbled.

And that was a lie. He had gotten everything. Perhaps not in the physical sense—though he would have had that, too, if Natalie hadn't burst in on them. But he took all she had to offer emotionally, and she had nothing left. She felt totally drained. At the moment, she couldn't feel anything, not even regret, though she knew that would come soon in bitter, drowning waves.

"I'm awfully tired, Natalie," she sighed. "I just want to go to sleep."

But sleep was not for her—not that night. Long after Natalie was asleep in the other bed, Jacquelyn stared up at the darkened ceiling. After a while she slipped out of bed, crept over to the heavy draperies and pulled them aside. The lights of Paris twinkled below.

She stood motionless, her gaze wandering over the city, her heart feeling dead and heavy in her chest. Was Natalie telling the truth? She went over every moment of the past hours that she had been with Scott. She searched her memory for one time Scott had mentioned the word "love" to her, but it was not there. She had been too dazzled by those shimmering hours to have questioned that at the time.

Jacquelyn felt tears bubbling up in her eyes. She stifled a sob that threatened to rip through her. As she gazed at the scene below her, she realized at last why Paris had captivated her so completely. She was in love with the city, true. But more than that, she was hopelessly in love with Scott McCrann. *Had* always loved him. *Would* always love him. No matter how ruthless he could be, no matter what he had done to Gerrard—and to her. There was a weakness in her where Scott was concerned that she could not fight. She could hide behind a shield of hate, tell herself that she was safe against Scott's appeal. But given the right time, the right moment, and his touch could set her on fire, melting all the resolve she had thought she possessed.

Face it, Jacquelyn, she told herself. *Where Scott McCrann is concerned, you are simply not to be trusted. He's done it to you before. He'll do it again, unless you take really drastic steps.*

A tear stole down her cheek, for she knew that no matter how deep her passion for Scott was, all she was ever going to have of him were the bittersweet memories of this one night. And now the memories were hot and fresh—the images of Scott and his unruly brown hair, his blue-eyed gaze hungrily roaming over her face, his lanky, lithe frame. She remembered how his arms felt when he slipped them around her, the warmth of his mouth on hers, the texture of his skin touching her bare, willing flesh.

A tingle ran down her spine. She closed her eyes and hugged the drapery close around her, sliding back and forth in its cool, soft lining, pretending it was Scott holding her.

But after a while the picture faded, and Jacquelyn had to face the cold reality that she was all alone and the cloth around her was only a feeble substitute for the man she loved.

But the cold, bitter fact remained that he didn't love her anymore. Desired her, yes. But love had died long ago when her refusal to marry him had killed the tenderness he had once felt, leaving only a bitter, angry desire in him to conquer and hurt her. Certainly if he had loved her he would have stood by her side and made it clear to Natalie tonight.

After they had returned to the States, his actions underscored the situation. He became engulfed in a whirlwind of business trips and activities, acting cold, preoccupied and withdrawn. He made no effort to clarify his feelings for her beyond what had happened between them that night.

It was a bitter pill for Jacquelyn to swallow but she had to admit it—Natalie had been right all along.

So she had made the decision to accept Austin's

proposal. It was the last defense she had left against a lifetime of heartbreak at the hands of a ruthless man who could take her at will and give nothing in return but regrets. Austin would never hurt her. He would cherish and care for her and protect her. And only Scott's memory could hurt her. For she was not the kind of woman who could be unfaithful to her husband. In time, the memory of Scott would fade. It would never leave, but she would be able to fit it into a secret compartment of her heart. She would not be the first woman to carry the memory of such a lost love with her all the days of her life.

In time, she would grow to love Austin. They would have a family. She would have a normal life.

"I've waited a long time, Jacquelyn," Austin said, taking her hand in his.

"Yes." Jacquelyn smiled. "Ever since we were children. I think the first time we had a pretend wedding was right here in the garden under that oak tree. We were eight years old."

Austin nodded. "I remember. It was a double ceremony. Natalie 'married' your brother, Gerrard. Both you girls wore old lace curtains for wedding gown trains."

"And we threw rice at each other that we'd stolen from Hattie's kitchen."

How poignant those memories were. How much happier all their lives would be now if Scott Mc-Crann had never entered them. The four of them would be married the way they'd planned as children, and probably with the same trusting innocence of children.

But a part of her did not regret that there was a chapter in her life called "Scott McCrann," for though it had left her with heartbreak, it had also left her with the memory of what the real love experience—the grand passion—was like. And that, at least, was more than some women ever experienced.

Perhaps the fates had decided it was enough for her. Perhaps the realization of such a love was too much for the cold imperfect realities of life.

She drew a deep breath, firmly putting those thoughts aside and coming to grips with the true moment. She held Austin's hands in hers, gazing directly into his eyes. "Austin, we've been too close for too many years for me ever to lie to you. You have to understand that although I have agreed to marry you, I'm not in love with you. I love you . . . but I'm not *in* love with you. Do you understand? Perhaps we've been so close for so many years that I feel a different kind of love for you, a tenderness, a companionship, a friendship. But I don't want to delude you."

He smiled crookedly. "Of course you're not deluding me, Jacquelyn. And I'm not deluding myself. Listen, some very successful marriages have been built on exactly the kind of friendship and understanding we have. I know we're going to be just fine together. And in time you'll know you did the right thing. We're going to have a good marriage."

Was he trying to convince her—or himself? she wondered afterward.

Jacquelyn broke the news to Scott the next day. They were sitting on the stone benches in the garden with the cool drapery of greenery surrounding them. The fountain, which had been repaired, now splashed softly.

From the direction of the roque court came the hard "smack" of a mallet against a ball. Uncle Luther and Austin were having an afternoon game.

Scott was relaxing with a mint julep and a cigar. "Everything is running very smoothly," he said, gesturing toward the white-columned mansion, which could be seen through the trees.

"Yes," Jacquelyn murmured absently.

Peace had settled over the great house after weeks of hectic activity by the army of carpenters. One remaining crew was finishing the trim work on the last wing of the mansion. Then it was just a matter of waiting until the final shipments of antiques arrived from Paris and her work would be completed. She should feel a great sense of accomplishment; the restoration of Cypress Halls was an outstanding success. Scott was enormously pleased and Uncle Luther was ecstatic. Already some national home and architectural magazines had contacted them about doing feature articles and photographic spreads on the house. But instead of savoring her achievement, Jacquelyn felt only a sense of emptiness.

"You seem quite preoccupied," Scott commented.

"Do I?"

She heard another crack of a ball on the roque court.

"Yes," Scott persisted. "You should be feeling quite pleased with yourself. The job you did on the mansion will be a feather in your professional cap."

From the roque court came a frustrated exclamation as Uncle Luther made a bad play.

She gathered her courage and said, "Well, I am pleased about that. In fact, I'm quite happy today, and not only because the restoration turned out so well." She paused. The afternoon seemed to grow still and oppressive. She said, "The main reason I'm happy is that I've agreed to marry Austin."

A pungent swear word sliced the air. Uncle Luther had lost the game.

For a moment, Scott seemed to have become a part of the stone bench on which he was seated. His cigar and drink hovered in midair. The lines around his mouth had grown deep and severe. His fingers whitened around the drink he was holding.

Oh, Scott, her heart cried out, *this is the moment of truth for us. It isn't too late. Tell me you love me and you refuse to let another man have me. Throw your cigar down. Swear and stomp around. Grab me by the shoulders and tell me I belong to you.*

The moment hung between them and then was gone forever. . . .

He rose slowly. His face seemed a bit pale, but he showed no other emotion. If some last shred of hope in her had cried out for a final testing, for the last convincing proof that Scott did not love her, she had it now.

The hope quietly died as Scott said, "Well, fine. I hope you and Austin will be very happy." He placed his drink on a garden table. For a moment he towered over Jacquelyn. There was a menacing quality about him that suddenly unnerved her. Was he furious that by accepting Austin's proposal she had outmaneuvered him and robbed him of the consummation of his revenge?

"Why don't we make it a double ceremony?" he suddenly said, his eyes overpowering her with their intensity.

"A double ceremony?" she echoed blankly.

"Yes. Natalie and I, too, are going to be married."

Chapter Nine

"Are you sure you're doing the right thing, Jacquelyn?"

"Of course, Aunt Perforce," Jacquelyn laughed.

She looked down at the stack of wedding invitations on the desk in front of her. Two piles—one for her and the other for Natalie. Aunt Perforce had just delivered the set of announcements she had helped Natalie address. Since she had raised Natalie and Austin, Aunt Perforce was taking on the duties normally relegated to a mother.

The older woman was giving Jacquelyn one of her typical searching, pessimistic looks. "I wonder," she murmured. "Have you really gotten Scott McCrann out of your system enough to marry another man?"

A flush stung Jacquelyn's cheeks. "Aunt Perforce! What a thing to say." She felt a mixture of exasperation and uneasiness. No one else on the face of the earth could be as blunt and outspoken as her eccentric aunt. The fact that the older woman was touching some nerve ends very close to Jacquelyn's heart did not help her emotional state.

"Well," declared Aunt Perforce, rising from her chair and preparing to leave, "I have some very uneasy vibrations about this situation. I'm going to spend the afternoon casting new horoscopes for you, Natalie and Austin. I hope the stars will reassure me by proving me wrong."

Jacquelyn suppressed a smile. "I'm sure the stars will tell you everything is going to be fine, Aunt Perforce," she said, though she knew from experience that her aunt never got anything but dire predictions from the stars.

Perhaps in this case they might be right, she thought with a sudden stab of pain.

But she brushed the dark thoughts aside just as quickly. No! She wasn't going to allow Aunt Perforce's gloomy mood to throw her into another state of depression. She had been all through that and had made a truce with her heart. A kind of quiet peace had taken the place of heartbreak. Perhaps it was resignation . . . accepting what life had finally given her. She was through with weeping over Scott McCrann and what might have been. That had been a dream from which she must awaken. Marriage to Austin and their life together was the reality she must occupy herself with now. She had plunged headlong into preparations for the giant formal wedding that would take place in the restored mansion.

Keeping busy day and night, she had discovered, was the very best antidote for a broken heart.

Having placed the last of the stamps on the invitations, Jacquelyn rose from her chair and stretched. As she headed for the mailbox with her bundle of invitations, she ran into Uncle Luther in the hallway.

"How's the bride-to-be?" he asked jovially.

"Fine, Uncle Luther." She smiled, putting on a cheerful expression.

"Just saw Perforce leave."

"Yes, she brought over some invitations she'd helped Natalie address."

"Well, it's good she's had something to do besides staring at those ridiculous astrological charts of hers all day. Poor woman isn't quite all there, you know." He tapped his temple with a significant gesture.

Jacquelyn suppressed a smile, remembering that Aunt Perforce had said exactly the same thing about Uncle Luther.

"You know, Jacquelyn," her uncle said, placing his long arm around her shoulder and walking with her toward the front of the mansion, "I don't know when I've been so happy."

"I've noticed the change in you," Jacquelyn said warmly.

"Yes, the arrangements you young people are making for this gala double wedding have been more beneficial to me than any medicine. To see Cypress Halls restored to its dignity and splendor and once again the center of a great social event has been a tonic for my old heart." He tapped his chest and smiled.

He went on, "I see that Scott is sparing no expense. He's invited notable people from all over the South—political figures, celebrities, people in the news. I was reading the guest list." He chuckled. "It looks like a string of pages out of *Who's Who*. Scott is flying in his favorite chef from Paris as well as an orchestra from New Orleans. Not since the pre–Civil War days, when the Cordoway family was in its heyday, has the mansion seen such an extravagant event."

Uncle Luther helped her place the invitations in the mailbox. "Ah, I see you're sending an invitation to Gerrard."

"Of course. You don't think I'd leave my own brother off the invitation list, do you?" she smiled.

"Well, I should hope not. Though I doubt if that young rascal will show up." He shook his head. "Don't mind telling you, Jacquelyn, that boy is something of a disappointment to me. Always had a wild streak in him. Caused me a lot of worry. He never did have his feet on the ground the way you did."

"He's been going through a rough time in his life, Uncle Luther," Jacquelyn said. She felt obliged to go to the defense of her brother, though she did not want to go into all the details of Gerrard's troubles. It was a matter best forgotten now.

"Yes, I suppose young men have their problems. Wouldn't hurt him to write me once in a while, though. Haven't heard a peep from him in months."

"Gerrard never was one for writing letters," Jacquelyn admitted.

"Well," said her uncle, brightening up, "let's take a stroll around the mansion. I just can't look enough at the beautiful job you've done on this place, my dear."

For a while, as they walked through the many

rooms and talked over old times, Jacquelyn felt a warm inner glow. For this moment, it was enough that Uncle Luther was in his glory.

Events began to pick up speed. Jacquelyn and Natalie spent several days in New Orleans making the final selection of their wedding dresses. They chose the flowers and decided on two wedding cakes. They made a decision on a mutual friend to sing at the ceremony. Jacquelyn made arrangements for the staff of servants who would see that the functions of the mansion ran smoothly.

For the present, she thought, she was the mistress of this beloved grand home of her ancestors. But one day it would become the property of Scott McCrann and his wife, Natalie. She tried not to think about that.

The rush and pressure of last-minute details were robbing her of a great deal of energy. Each night she fell into bed, too exhausted to think. She became caught up in a tailspin of emotional frenzy—so much so that it was a shock to her when she looked on the calendar one morning and saw that only two days remained before the ceremony.

That night there was a quiet family dinner, which would no doubt be the last peaceful moment for them until the wedding was over. Natalie and Austin had joined Jacquelyn and Uncle Luther for the meal. Scott had been called to New Orleans on a business matter and was away for the evening.

They discussed the final wedding preparations over the meal and afterward had coffee and brandy in the restored library of the great house.

Jacquelyn heard Hattie go to answer a knock at

the front door. She heard an exclamation of surprise from Hattie, then a man's voice. Conversation in the room halted. Eyes turned toward the man standing in the doorway.

Jacquelyn's eyes widened. Her breath caught in her throat. For a second she couldn't trust herself to believe what she was seeing. Then she put her cup down with a clatter and jumped to her feet. "Gerrard!" she cried, and ran into her brother's arms.

She was lifted off her feet and swung around. "Sis!" cried a laughing, deeply tanned Gerrard.

"You're squeezing the breath out of me!" she gasped. "Put me down and let me look at you."

She took two steps backward, gazing at her brother with disbelief. "Gerrard, is it really you?"

"A good question. The tall man before her resembled her brother. But the change in him took some readjusting on her part. He seemed a foot taller, his shoulders much wider. The Gerrard she remembered had been a slender young man with nervous mannerisms and a pale, aristocratic face that had a bit of a look of dissipation about it. That Gerrard had been a boy compared to the husky man who stood before her now. He'd gained at least thirty pounds, and from the feel of his arms and shoulders, all of it was muscle. His eyes were bright and clear. She realized the reason he looked taller was that he stood so straight and held his chin high and proud.

"Gerrard, my boy." Uncle Luther crossed the room in long strides, extending a hand.

Gerrard shook the hand warmly, gazing into his uncle's eyes. And then, with a sudden impulse, he hugged his uncle, patting his shoulders with a display of emotion that strong men can show one another. Jacquelyn's eyes filled with tears at this warm reunion between her brother and uncle.

Next Austin stepped forward and greeted Gerrard.

Jacquelyn was suddenly aware of a break in the excited stream of greetings. She saw Gerrard looking across the room. She followed his gaze and saw a pale Natalie, who had risen to her feet and was standing like a frozen statue beside the fireplace mantel. The entire room seemed to dissolve into a stage setting for the look that passed between them.

Gerrard slowly crossed the room and took her hand. "Natalie," he said softly, "I want to wish you all the happiness in the world."

She swallowed, looked up at him and seemed to be fighting back tears. Her voice was barely audible when she said, "Thank you, Gerrard."

Later that evening, Gerrard and Jacquelyn took a stroll around the mansion grounds. Moonlight bathed the lawns and trees in silver. From the distant swamp came the soft warble of a night bird. Behind them, the mansion was aglow with lights.

"I can't believe my own eyes," Gerrard exclaimed. "It's simply incredible what you all have done with that old house. When I left, it was in ruins. Now it's like walking into a page of *Gone With the Wind*. The old plantation mansion restored in all its elegance."

"It's been quite a task, but well worth it," Jacquelyn said.

"Uncle Luther's lifelong dream come true. I think it's just great."

They reached the garden and sat near the fountain.

"Why didn't you let us know you were coming?" Jacquelyn demanded.

"I thought it would be fun to surprise you."

"Well, you certainly did that. Just about made me faint."

They both laughed.

"But I'm glad you're here," she continued. "I was secretly praying my brother would be here to see me get married. But I wasn't holding out a whole lot of hope."

"You and Austin." Gerrard smiled. "After all these years." He paused, glancing around the garden. Then he said slowly, "Remember when we were kids playing here? You had plenty of rehearsals for this wedding. You and Austin were always playing pretend wedding. And Natalie and I—" His voice suddenly broke off. A shadow crossed his face.

Jacquelyn touched his hand. "Any regrets, Gerrard?" she asked softly.

He smiled sadly. "Perhaps a few, Sis." He drew a deep breath, straightening his shoulders. "But that's water under the bridge, isn't it? I'm just here to see my sister and my old friends get married . . . not to go stirring up old memories."

She changed the subject. "Listen, I want to hear what you've been doing. I certainly didn't get much information from those few scrawled cards you sent me."

"Well, you know me and writing letters. Anyway, too much has happened to me to ever put in a letter. I don't exactly know where to begin, Sis. I have a whole new life now."

"Whatever you've been up to, it sure has agreed with you. You look simply wonderful, Gerrard, so strong and healthy."

"That's from the hard physical outdoor work I'm doing with a lumber company in Oregon. You know," he chuckled, "I never was one for exerting myself much when I was living around here, except for lifting a glass in a bar or driving too fast in the car Uncle Luther bought me."

"You were a bit of a rounder," Jacquelyn admitted.

He became serious. "Well, all that's changed. I've been working hard, saving my money. I bought a small mobile home to live in and fixed it up real nice. You and Austin will have to come visit me up there. It's really beautiful, Jacquelyn—the mountains, the forests—it brought me to a whole new dimension in myself that I'd never known before."

"I'm so glad, Gerrard. You don't know how much I worried about you."

He nodded soberly. "I know how much grief I caused you and Uncle Luther. That last night I saw you in New Orleans I'd really hit rock bottom. I hitchhiked out to California, staying drunk most of the time. I can't remember a lot of what I did or where I went. But one night I found myself in a mission for bums and down-and-outers."

"Oh, Gerrard . . . !"

"Yeah, it was the pits all right. But that was what I needed, Sis. Sometimes a person in my condition has to go to the very bottom before he can face what he's doing to his life and try to start climbing back up.

"This mission was one of those little storefront dumps where you could get a free meal, a bath and a bed for the night if you were willing to sit through one of their preaching services. As I sat there, only half listening to the sermon, something happened to me. I looked around at the human derelicts, the poor, sick creatures throwing their lives away on drugs and booze. A cold chill came over me when I realized with a shock that I was looking at myself. I don't know what happened to me, but I came out of that place a changed person. I guess for the first time I saw clearly where I was headed, and it scared the heck out of me.

"Anyway, I hitched a ride up to Oregon where I landed a job with the lumber company. At first I thought the hard work was going to kill me, but after a while I loved it. I haven't had a drink since that night in California. I've come to the realization that I have to accept responsibility for my own failures. I have to stop blaming other people for my mistakes, like the way I blamed Scott McCrann for causing my lumber business here to fail."

Jacquelyn felt a cold draft. She looked at her brother with stricken eyes. "But—but it was Scott's fault, wasn't it? You told me he used unfair business tactics to deliberately run you out of business."

"I know that's what I told you, Jacquelyn. And I guess I honestly believed it at the time. At least, I'd convinced myself it was true. But I know now it was a cop-out on my part, a rationalization. I just didn't want to face the truth that I'd failed because of my own shortcomings as a businessman, my own inexperience. I had too much pride to face the truth. So I tried to blame it all on someone else, then go hide in a bottle."

Jacquelyn tried to swallow, but the pain in her throat was too intense. She felt stunned, incapable of clear thought. In a weak voice, she said, "Then you're telling me that Scott didn't really deliberately set out to bankrupt you—that he didn't resort to unethical business dealings?"

Gerrard shook his head. "Now that I can face the truth, I realize that just wasn't true. Scott McCrann is a very sharp businessman and a tough competitor. But he's never done anything unethical in his life, Sis. My business failed because of my own incompetence, nothing more. I just didn't have what it takes to compete with someone as good as Scott McCrann."

"But—but you said he was responsible for the bank not giving you a loan!"

"That's what I made myself believe. But look at the facts. I was the worst credit risk in town. Everybody around here knew how irresponsible I was. I had no collateral. My lumber business was on the rocks. Poor Uncle Luther was against the wall financially. Why, no sensible banker in his right mind would have given me the kind of loan I was asking for. And if they had, it wouldn't have made any difference in the long run." He shook his head. "I'm ashamed to admit it, Sis, but at least I'm man enough now to face the truth. I was like a spoiled kid losing a ball game who had to yell 'foul' because he blew the game."

The night closed around Jacquelyn like a suffocating blanket. Her mind was spinning in several different directions at the same time. She tried to regain a grasp on her chaotic thoughts while fighting hard to keep her emotions under control.

One thought was hammering at her with devastating force. There had been no real basis for her anger at Scott. He'd been innocent all along of the cruel revenge on her brother of which she'd believed him guilty. He wasn't underhanded and vindictive at all. He had been falsely accused.

Then why had it seemed that he was vengeful toward her? He had tried to have an affair with her in Paris, hadn't he? And he'd said nothing about love or marriage. It had been purely a masculine conquest, a male ego trip—or at least it had certainly appeared that way to her. Had it grown out of his injured pride?

Of course he could not have known why she had been so angry and bitter toward him—an anger and bitterness that had grown out of her mistaken idea about his destroying Gerrard's business. Not knowing that, he would have gone on interpreting her coldness as simply a rejection of him as a suitor. That would have been enough to sting the pride of any strong man. And perhaps could have made him want to conquer her, if only for one night.

Tears blinded her. How ironic fate was, for her to discover the truth now that it was too late. She felt an hysterical urge to laugh at this grotesque joke life had played on them all.

She knew she should be furious at Gerrard. But she couldn't even find it in her heart to feel that. He hadn't deliberately deceived her about Scott. At the time, he was deceiving himself, too blinded by self-pity and wounded pride to admit the truth. Anyway, he'd believed that Jacquelyn and Scott had broken up, so he couldn't have known he was destroying a chance they might have had for patching up their broken romance.

Maybe there was something to Aunt Perforce's horoscopes. If so, they had all been born under unlucky stars. How the fates must be laughing at them all. She was marrying Austin, a man she didn't really love. Natalie was marrying Scott McCrann, but she was still obviously carrying a torch for Gerrard. Jacquelyn had seen that clearly spelled out in Natalie's eyes when she came face to face with Gerrard last night. And Gerrard still cared for her, too.

What a tragic ending to their childhood dreams. But that was often the fate childhood dreams came to, wasn't it?

She couldn't force herself to carry on any further conversation. She excused herself, blaming her state of exhaustion on the wedding preparations, and went to her room, where she knew she'd soak her pillow with hopeless tears of regret.

Chapter Ten

Cypress Halls greeted the arriving guests with haughty dignity. She was a great lady, a fallen queen who had been restored to her rightful throne, and she gloried in the reclamation of all her splendor.

Jacquelyn looked out her bedroom window. It was too bright a day for such a heavy heart.

A long sleek car pulled into the horseshoe driveway carrying more guests coming for the wedding and the great banquet reception that was to follow.

A tap at the door; Jacquelyn turned as the door opened. A billowing white cascade of lace and ruffles floated in. It moved toward her like the specter of an antebellum plantation belle. Jacquelyn had deliberately chosen a style reminiscent of the hoop skirt and corset era to match the setting of Cypress Halls, furnished now almost entirely with nineteenth-century antiques.

The long, flowing wedding dress inched its way to

the closet door and hooked itself on a hanger attached to the outside. Then Hattie peeked from behind the yards of fabric.

"There," she said. "That ought to do it. "It's perfect down to the last detail. Not a wrinkle anywhere, and every ruffle crisp and proud."

"Thank you, Hattie." Jacquelyn fingered the delicate white lace bordering the long sleeves. Hattie helped her dress. Excitement was in the air. It flowed from room to room throughout the mansion. From downstairs came the strains of a string ensemble, playing as guests began being seated in the spacious ballroom where the wedding would take place.

"I declare!" Hattie exclaimed. "I'm all thumbs. Stuck myself a half dozen times with a pin. I don't know when I've been so excited. It's like a dream come true, all the flowers and decorations, that big banquet table, those famous people Scott invited. Do you know I saw two movie stars and an ex-governor? It's just like a story on television!"

Jacquelyn smiled faintly. She turned to stand before the full-length mirror and saw the pale oval of her face reflected.

"Oh, honey," Hattie whispered, "you're just the most beautiful bride in the world." She began sniffling. "You've got to forgive a blubbery old woman," she choked, dabbing at her eyes with her apron. "But you're the same as my own little girl, you know. And now I'm seein' my little girl all grown up and so beautiful on her wedding day. . . ."

Jacquelyn turned to embrace the housekeeper whom she had loved so many years. Hattie's work-gnarled hands patted her clumsily as they both wept.

Then Hattie said, "Now you've gone and smeared

your makeup. If we keep this up, your dress will be ruined." She gave Jacquelyn another pat and fled from the room.

Jacquelyn faced the mirror again repairing her face. Her stomach was beginning to flutter. She was caught up in the tension and excitement of the moment, her pulse racing, her hands icy. Bride's jitters combined with stage fright, she thought.

Beyond that, she was not allowing herself to feel anything. Last night she had shed the last of her tears and put the broken dreams to rest. There was simply no going back to undo the past at this late date. She had resigned herself to accepting what life had given her. Now, in a few minutes, she would be walking down the aisle on Uncle Luther's arm and would become Mrs. Austin D'Raulde before a packed ballroom of hundreds of guests.

The door opened again. Jacquelyn turned, surprised to see Natalie. Then her eyes widened. "Natalie! What are you doing in those clothes? Shouldn't you be putting on your wedding dress? We're supposed to be downstairs in a few minutes."

Natalie was wearing a simple white linen street dress. She stepped into the room, closed the door, then leaned back against it, her eyes wide and dark in her pale face.

Jacquelyn moved closer to her with a rustle of her dress. "Natalie, whatever is it? You look so strange. Are you sick?"

Natalie shook her head. "No. Just scared."

"I understand. I feel the same way. What bride wouldn't, getting married like this with all those people watching—"

"That's not the reason I'm scared."

"Then I guess I don't understand."

Natalie was clasping her hands nervously. "Oh, Jackie, I'm about to do something absolutely insane. Please tell me I'm doing the right thing. No, you don't have to tell me. I know it's the right thing, but—"

"You're not making a whole lot of sense, Natalie," Jacquelyn said, looking at her friend with growing concern. "Are you sure you're all right?"

"Yes, I guess so. I mean, I will be all right . . . soon. But I'm sure going to cause a scandal."

"Scandal?" Jacquelyn echoed.

"Yes. I'm going to elope."

Jacquelyn stared at her blankly for a moment. Then she exploded, "Natalie, you have taken leave of your senses! Elope, with all those guests downstairs? How could Scott think of doing such a thing? Most of those people are friends he invited. He's spent a fortune on this wedding—"

"No, you don't understand," Natalie said desperately. "I'm not eloping with Scott. I'm not going to marry Scott. I'm going to elope with Gerrard."

There was a moment of utter, stunned silence.

Finally, Jacquelyn said, "Hattie told me she'd kill me if I sat down in this dress, but under the circumstances, I think she'd forgive me." She collapsed on the side of the bed.

She sat there for a moment, trying to make her frozen thought processes operate. Would you repeat what you just told me?" she asked weakly.

"I said, I'm not going to marry Scott. I am going to run off with your brother, Gerrard, and get married."

Jacquelyn shook her head, utterly dazed. "When on earth did you make this decision?"

"I guess I made it the moment Gerrard walked

into the room where we all were night before last. The minute I saw him, I knew how much I still loved him. I knew I didn't love Scott at all. I'd gone to him on the rebound. Partly, I suppose, it was that old competition between you and me, Jackie. You see, I always felt inferior around you. You were the one with the great personality, the talent, the family background. I envied you. Taking Scott away from you was a way of winning over you."

A half-hysterical laugh broke from Jacquelyn's lips. "And I always blamed myself for being secretly jealous of you because you are so beautiful!"

They stared tearfully at each other, then Natalie rushed into Jacquelyn's arms. "Oh, Jackie," she sobbed, "I do love you in spite of everything."

"And I love you, Natalie. Just the way I did when we were children."

Then she dried her eyes. "Now for heaven's sake, tell me what has taken place between you and Gerrard."

"Well, we've had several long talks since he came back. You see, I was so hurt, so angry when he just walked out of my life that way. I didn't think I could ever forgive him for leaving me that way. He didn't even say good-bye. But he explained all that: how ashamed he was, how he had considered himself a failure, the crisis he was going through in his life. Now I understand, and I've forgiven him. The more we talked, the more we realized how much in love we still were with each other. Finally, just a little while ago, Gerrard told me he couldn't stand by and see me marry Scott. He begged me to elope with him, and I have just agreed to do it. I know it's the right thing. Scott won't be hurt because he doesn't really love me. It's you he loves, Jacquelyn. He's never gotten you out of his system. I tried to kid myself into believing he had. But deep down, I knew better. And I know you still love him, too. The trouble is, both of you are so stubborn and so filled with pride that you won't admit it to each other!''

Natalie grasped Jacquelyn's hands tightly in hers, gazing directly at her. ''Jackie, don't you make a terrible mistake, either. Don't marry Austin. It's not fair to Scott. It's not fair to you. And most of all, it wouldn't be fair to Austin. In a few more minutes it's going to be too late. Don't let that happen.''

''I—I wish I could believe you, Natalie. About Scott being in love with me. But that time in Paris, he never once said anything about love or marriage to me. After we came back he was so cold and distant. It was obvious he just wanted to get me in bed to satisfy his male ego.''

Natalie shook her head. ''It's his pride, I tell you. I wouldn't admit it to you before because we were two women fighting for the same man. The truth is, Scott was fighting himself. He does still care for you, but he's too stubborn to admit it. I can be truthful with you now, Jackie. Don't let his pigheadedness keep the two of you apart. You belong together. Fight for him, Jackie. Make him admit he loves you.''

Jacquelyn swallowed hard. ''But Natalie . . . your brother . . . Austin. He's waiting right now to go meet me at the altar.''

''Then go have a talk with him. Tell him the truth. That's much kinder than marrying him under these circumstances. He'll be hurt at first, but he'll get over it. Listen, I know Austin. After all, he's my brother. He's had this childhood dream of marrying you and just can't let go. He's more in love with the dream than he really is with you. He knows you

Silhouette Romance

IT'S YOUR OWN SPECIAL TIME

Contemporary romances for today's women.
Each month, six very special love stories will be yours
from SILHOUETTE. Look for them wherever books are sold
or order now from the coupon below.

$1.50 each

☐ 5 Goforth	☐ 28 Hampson	☐ 54 Beckman	☐ 83 Halston
☐ 6 Stanford	☐ 29 Wildman	☐ 55 LaDame	☐ 84 Vitek
☐ 7 Lewis	☐ 30 Dixon	☐ 56 Trent	☐ 85 John
☐ 8 Beckman	☐ 32 Michaels	☐ 57 John	☐ 86 Adams
☐ 9 Wilson	☐ 33 Vitek	☐ 58 Stanford	☐ 87 Michaels
☐ 10 Caine	☐ 34 John	☐ 59 Vernon	☐ 88 Stanford
☐ 11 Vernon	☐ 35 Stanford	☐ 60 Hill	☐ 89 James
☐ 17 John	☐ 38 Browning	☐ 61 Michaels	☐ 90 Major
☐ 19 Thornton	☐ 39 Sinclair	☐ 62 Halston	☐ 92 McKay
☐ 20 Fulford	☐ 46 Stanford	☐ 63 Brent	☐ 93 Browning
☐ 22 Stephens	☐ 47 Vitek	☐ 71 Ripy	☐ 94 Hampson
☐ 23 Edwards	☐ 48 Wildman	☐ 73 Browning	☐ 95 Wisdom
☐ 24 Healy	☐ 49 Wisdom	☐ 76 Hardy	☐ 96 Beckman
☐ 25 Stanford	☐ 50 Scott	☐ 78 Oliver	☐ 97 Clay
☐ 26 Hastings	☐ 52 Hampson	☐ 81 Roberts	☐ 98 St. George
☐ 27 Hampson	☐ 53 Browning	☐ 82 Dailey	☐ 99 Camp

$1.75 each

☐ 100 Stanford	☐ 110 Trent	☐ 120 Carroll	☐ 130 Hardy
☐ 101 Hardy	☐ 111 South	☐ 121 Langan	☐ 131 Stanford
☐ 102 Hastings	☐ 112 Stanford	☐ 122 Scofield	☐ 132 Wisdom
☐ 103 Cork	☐ 113 Browning	☐ 123 Sinclair	☐ 133 Rowe
☐ 104 Vitek	☐ 114 Michaels	☐ 124 Beckman	☐ 134 Charles
☐ 105 Eden	☐ 115 John	☐ 125 Bright	☐ 135 Logan
☐ 106 Dailey	☐ 116 Lindley	☐ 126 St. George	☐ 136 Hampson
☐ 107 Bright	☐ 117 Scott	☐ 127 Roberts	☐ 137 Hunter
☐ 108 Hampson	☐ 118 Dailey	☐ 128 Hampson	☐ 138 Wilson
☐ 109 Vernon	☐ 119 Hampson	☐ 129 Converse	☐ 139 Vitek

$1.75 each

☐ 140 Erskine	☐ 161 Trent	☐ 181 Terrill	☐ 201 Starr
☐ 142 Browning	☐ 162 Ashby	☐ 182 Clay	☐ 202 Hampson
☐ 143 Roberts	☐ 163 Roberts	☐ 183 Stanley	☐ 203 Browning
☐ 144 Goforth	☐ 164 Browning	☐ 184 Hardy	☐ 204 Carroll
☐ 145 Hope	☐ 165 Young	☐ 185 Hampson	☐ 205 Maxam
☐ 146 Michaels	☐ 166 Wisdom	☐ 186 Howard	☐ 206 Manning
☐ 147 Hampson	☐ 167 Hunter	☐ 187 Scott	☐ 207 Windham
☐ 148 Cork	☐ 168 Carr	☐ 188 Cork	☐ 208 Halston
☐ 149 Saunders	☐ 169 Scott	☐ 189 Stephens	☐ 209 LaDame
☐ 150 Major	☐ 170 Ripy	☐ 190 Hampson	☐ 210 Eden
☐ 151 Hampson	☐ 171 Hill	☐ 191 Browning	☐ 211 Walters
☐ 152 Halston	☐ 172 Browning	☐ 192 John	☐ 212 Young
☐ 153 Dailey	☐ 173 Camp	☐ 193 Trent	☐ 213 Dailey
☐ 154 Beckman	☐ 174 Sinclair	☐ 194 Barry	☐ 214 Hampson
☐ 155 Hampson	☐ 175 Jarrett	☐ 195 Dailey	☐ 215 Roberts
☐ 156 Sawyer	☐ 176 Vitek	☐ 196 Hampson	☐ 216 Saunders
☐ 157 Vitek	☐ 177 Dailey	☐ 197 Summers	☐ 217 Vitek
☐ 158 Reynolds	☐ 178 Hampson	☐ 198 Hunter	☐ 218 Hunter
☐ 159 Tracy	☐ 179 Beckman	☐ 199 Roberts	☐ 219 Cork
☐ 160 Hampson	☐ 180 Roberts	☐ 200 Lloyd	

$1.95 each

_#220 THE DAWN IS GOLDEN, Hampson	_#226 SWEET SECOND LOVE, Hampson
_#221 PRACTICAL DREAMER, Browning	_#227 FORBIDDEN AFFAIR, Beckman
_#222 TWO FACES OF LOVE, Carroll	_#228 DANCE AT YOUR WEDDING, King
_#223 A PRIVATE EDEN, Summers	_#229 FOR ERIC'S SAKE, Thornton
_#224 HIDDEN ISLE, Langan	_#230 IVORY INNOCENCE, Stevens
_#225 DELTA RIVER MAGIC, St. George	_#231 WESTERN MAN, Dailey

----

SILHOUETTE BOOKS, Department SB/1
1230 Avenue of the Americas
New York, NY 10020

Please send me the books I have checked above. I am enclosing $_____
(please add 50¢ to cover postage and handling. NYS and NYC residents please
add appropriate sales tax). Send check or money order—no cash or C.O.D's
please. Allow six weeks for delivery.

NAME _____

ADDRESS _____

CITY _____ STATE/ZIP _____

Coming next month from
Silhouette Romances

Spell Of The Island by Anne Hampson

Emma went to Mauritius to rescue her sister, only to have her own heart captured by the handsome Paul Fanchotte—a man who had vowed to never give his heart to any woman!

Edge Of Paradise by Dorothy Vernon

It would be easy to go along with the hoax and play Paul's adoring lover by day. But how would Catherine survive the night without the warmth of his strong arms?

Next Year's Blonde by Joan Smith

Was it wise to trust Simon, a man accustomed to using his devastating charm to get anything he wanted? Prudent or not, Tillie willingly risked all to find out.

No Easy Conquest by Arlene James

Did Nicholas Boudreaux, the man who had first admired Josie's work, really believe she had talent? Or had he lured her to New Orleans for his own selfish reasons?

Lost In Love by Mia Maxam

From the moment Miranda felt the handsome stranger's arm slide around her, she knew how wonderful things would be if they were really man and wife, and not just pretending!

Winter Promise by Fran Wilson

Three years ago Kurt had pledged his love; a promise he never kept. Now Colby found herself falling in love all over again. Could she make Kurt remember the love she'd never forget?

Silhouette Romance

15-Day Free Trial Offer
6 Silhouette Romances

6 Silhouette Romances, free for 15 days! We'll send you 6 new Silhouette Romances to keep for 15 days, absolutely free! If you decide not to keep them, send them back to us. You pay nothing.

Free Home Delivery. But if you enjoy them as much as we think you will, keep them by paying the invoice enclosed with your free trial shipment. We'll pay all shipping and handling charges. You get the convenience of Home Delivery and we pay the postage and handling charge each month.

Don't miss a copy. The Silhouette Book Club is the way to make sure you'll be able to receive every new romance we publish before they're sold out. There is no minimum number of books to buy and you can cancel at any time.

This offer expires December 31, 1983